JASMINE

JASMINE

Bharati Mukherjee

Grove Weidenfeld
New York

Copyright © 1989 by Bharati Mukherjee

Published by Grove Weidenfeld
a division of Wheatland Corporation
841 Broadway
New York, N.Y. 10003-4793

Library of Congress Cataloging-in-Publication Data

Mukherjee, Bharati.
    Jasmine / by Bharati Mukherjee. — 1st ed.
        p.   cm.
    ISBN 0-8021-1032-0 (alk. paper)
    I. Title.
    PR9499.3.M77J3   1989
    813'.54—dc20   89-7611
                                           CIP

Designed by Paul Chevannes

Manufactured in the United States of America

This book is printed on acid-free paper

First Edition 1989

1   3   5   7   9   10   8   6   4   2

For Jim Harris, ardent Hawkeye

The new geometry mirrors a universe that is rough, not rounded, scabrous, not smooth. It is a geometry of the pitted, pocked, and broken up, the twisted, tangled, and intertwined.

James Gleick, *Chaos*

JASMINE

1

Lifetimes ago, under a banyan tree in the village of Hasnapur, an astrologer cupped his ears—his satellite dish to the stars—and foretold my widowhood and exile. I was only seven then, fast and venturesome, scabrous-armed from leaves and thorns.

"No!" I shouted. "You're a crazy old man. You don't know what my future holds!"

"Suit yourself," the astrologer cackled. "What is to happen will happen." Then he chucked me hard on the head.

I fell. My teeth cut into my tongue. A twig sticking out of the bundle of firewood I'd scavenged punched a star-shaped wound into my forehead. I lay still. The astrologer re-entered his trance. I was nothing, a speck in the solar system. Bad times were on their way. I was helpless, doomed. The star bled.

"I don't believe you," I whispered.

The astrologer folded up his tattered mat and pushed his feet into rubber sandals. "Fate is Fate. When Behula's bridegroom was fated to die of snakebite on their wedding night, did building a steel fortress prevent his death? A magic snake will penetrate solid walls when necessary."

I smelled the sweetness of winter wildflowers. Quails hopped, hiding and seeking me in the long grass. Squirrels as tiny as mice swished over my arms, dropping nuts. The trees were stooped and gnarled, as though the ghosts of old women had taken root. I always felt the she-ghosts were guarding me. I didn't feel I was nothing.

"Go join your sisters," the man with the capacious ears commanded. "A girl shouldn't be wandering here by herself." He pulled me to my feet and pointed to the trail that led out of the woods to the river bend.

I dragged my bundle to the river bend. I hated that river bend. The water pooled there, sludgy brown, and was choked with hyacinths and feces from the buffaloes that village boys washed upstream. Women were scouring brass pots with ashes. Dhobis were whomping clothes clean on stone slabs. Housewives squabbled while lowering their pails into a drying well. My older sisters, slow, happy girls with butter-smooth arms, were still bathing on the steps that led down to the river.

"What happened?" my sisters shrieked as they sponged the bleeding star on my forehead with the wetted ends of their veils. "Now your face is scarred for life! How will the family ever find you a husband?"

I broke away from their solicitous grip. "It's not a scar," I shouted, "it's my third eye." In the stories that our mother recited, the holiest sages developed an extra eye right in the middle of their foreheads. Through that eye they peered out into invisible worlds. "Now I'm a sage."

My sisters scampered up the slippery steps, grabbed their pitchers and my bundle of firewood, and ran to get help from the women at the well.

I swam to where the river was a sun-gold haze. I kicked and paddled in a rage. Suddenly my fingers scraped the soft waterlogged carcass of a small dog. The body was rotten, the eyes had been eaten. The moment I touched it, the body broke in two, as though the water had been its glue. A stench leaked out of the broken body, and then both pieces quickly sank.

That stench stays with me. I'm twenty-four now, I live in Baden, Elsa County, Iowa, but every time I lift a glass of water to my lips, fleetingly I smell it. I know what I don't want to become.

2

TAYLOR didn't want me to run away to Iowa. How can anyone leave New York, he said, how can *you* leave New York, you belong here. Iowa's dull and it's flat, he said.

So is Punjab, I said.

You deserve better.

There are many things I deserve, not all of them better. Taylor thought dull was the absence of action, but dull is its own kind of action. Dullness is a kind of luxury.

Taylor was wrong. Iowa isn't flat, not Elsa County.

It's a late May afternoon in a dry season and sunlight crests the hillocks like sea foam, then angles across the rolling sea of Lutzes' ground before snagging on the maples and box elders at the far end of ours. The Lutzes and Ripplemeyers' fifteen hundred acres cut across a dozen ponds and glacial moraines, back to back in a six-mile swath. The Ripplemeyer land: Bud's and mine and Du's. Jane Ripplemeyer has a bank account. So does Jyoti Vijh, in a different city. Bud's father started the First Bank of Baden above the barber's; now Bud runs it out of a smart low building between Kwik Copy and the new Drug Town.

Bud wants me to marry him, "officially," he says, before the baby comes. People assume we're married. He's a small-town banker, he's not allowed to do impulsive things. I'm less than half his age, and very foreign. We're the kind who marry. Going for me is this: he wasn't in a wheelchair when we met. I didn't leave him after it happened.

From the kitchen I can see the only Lutz boy, Darrel, work the ground. Darrel looks lost these days, like a little boy, inside the double-wide, air-conditioned cab of a monster tractor. Gene Lutz weighed nearly three hundred pounds and needed every square inch.

This is Darrel's first planting alone. The wheels of his tractor are plumed with dust as fine as talcum. The contour-plowed fields are quilts in shades of pale green and dry brown. Closer in, where our ground slopes into the Lutzes', Shadow, Darrel's huge black dog, picks his way through ankle-high tufts of corn. A farm dog knows not to damage leaves, even when it races ahead after a weasel or a field mouse. The topsoil rising from Shadow's paws looks like pockets of smoke.

Last winter Gene and Carol Lutz went to California as they usually did in January, after the money was in and before the taxes were due, and Gene, who was fifty-four years old, choked to death on a piece of Mexican food. He was so heavy Carol couldn't lift him to do the Heimlich maneuver. The waiters were all illegals who went into hiding as soon as the police were called.

Gene looked after everything for me when Bud was in the hospital. Now Bud wants to do the same for Darrel and the Lutz farm, but he's not the man he once was. I can look out Mother Ripplemeyer's back window and not see to the end of our small empire of ownership. Gene used to say to Bud, "Put our farms smack in the middle of the Loop and we'd about reach from Wrigley to Comiskey."

In our three and a half years together, I have given Bud a new trilogy to contemplate: Brahma, Vishnu, and Shiva. And he has lent me his: Musial, Brock, and Gibson. Bud's father grew up in southern Iowa, and Gene's father came from Davenport. Ottumwa got Cardinal broadcasts, and Davenport got the Cubs. Baseball loyalties are passed from fathers to sons. Bud says he's a Cardinals banker in Cubbie land. He favors speed and execution: he'll lend to risk takers who'll plant new crops and try new methods. Gene Lutz went with proven power: corn, beans, and hogs. After a good year, he'd buy himself the latest gadget from the implement dealer: immense tractors with air-conditioned cabs, equipped with stereo tape deck. A typical Cubbie tractor, Bud would joke, all power and no mobility—but he approved the purchase anyhow. Gene even painted an official Cubs logo on its side. I thought it said *Ubs.* Darrel painted the Hawkeye logo over it.

Darrel has a sister out in San Diego, married to a naval officer. Carol moved to be near her. With all the old Iowans in Southern California, she does not think she'll be a widow for long. Darrel had a girl living with him last fall, but she left for Texas after the first Alberta Clipper.

Darrel talks of selling, and I don't blame him. A thousand acres is too much for someone who graduated from Northern Iowa just last summer. He'd like to go to New Mexico, he says, and open up a franchise, away from the hogs and cold and farmer's hours. Radio Shack, say. He's only a year younger than I, but I cannot guess his idea of reality. I treat him as an innocent.

Yesterday he came over for dinner. People are getting used to some of my concoctions, even if they make a show of fanning their mouths. They get disappointed if there's not *something* Indian on the table. Last summer Darrel sent away to California for "Oriental herb garden" cuttings and planted some things for me—coriander, mainly, and dill weed, fenugreek and about five kinds of chili peppers. I always make sure to use his herbs.

Last night he said that two fellows had come up from Dalton in Johnson County with plans for putting in a golf course on his father's farm. Bud told me later that the fellows from Dalton are big developers. With ground so cheap and farmers so desperate, they're snapping up huge packages for future non-ag use. Airfields and golf courses and water slides and softball parks. It breaks Bud's heart even to mention it.

Darrel's pretty worked up about it. They'd have night golf with illuminated fairways. Wednesday nights would be Ladies' Nights, Thursday nights Stags Only, Friday nights for Couples. They're copying some kind of golf-course franchise that works out West. The plan is to convert the barn into a clubhouse, with a restaurant and what he calls sports facilities. I'm not sure what they'll do with the pig house and its built-in reservoir of nightsoil.

"If you're so set on sticking with a golf course," Bud said, "why don't you buy the franchise yourself?"

"I couldn't stand watching folks tramping down my fields," he said.

"So, what'll you call the club?" I asked Darrel. It didn't seem such a bad idea. A water slide, a nighttime golf course, tennis courts inside the weathered, slanting barn.

"The Barn," Darrel said. "I was hoping you'd come up with a prettier name. Something in Indian." He started blushing. I want to say to Darrel, "You mean in Hindi, not Indian, there's no such thing as Indian," but he'll be crushed and won't say anything for the rest of the night. He comes from a place where the language you speak is what you are.

The farmers around here are like the farmers I grew up with. Modest people, never boastful, tactful and courtly in their way. A farmer is dependent on too many things outside his control; it makes for modesty. They're hemmed in by etiquette. When they break out of it, like Harlan Kroener did, you know how terrible things have gotten.

Baden is what they call a basic German community. Even the Danes and Swedes are thought to be genetically unpredictable at times. I've heard the word "inscrutable." The inscrutable Swedes. The sneaky Dutch. They aren't Amish, but they're very fond of old ways of doing things. They're conservative people with a worldly outlook.

At dinner, Bud snapped Darrel's head off. "What farmer is nuts enough to golf three or four nights a week around here?" he asked.

Darrel tried to joke about it. "Times change. Farmers change. Even Wrigley's getting lights, Bud."

Bud's probably right. Most times he's right. But being right, having to point out the cons when the borrower wants to hear only the pros, is eating him up. He pops his stomach pills, on top of everything else. Blood pressure, diuretics, all sorts of skin creams. Immobility has made him more excitable. Later that night I tried to calm him down. I said, "Darrel won't have to sell. You'll see, it'll rain." Then I took his big pink hand, speckled with golden age spots and silky with reddish blond hairs, and placed it on my stomach. His hair is bushy and mostly white, but once upon a time he was a strawberry blond with bright blue eyes. The eyes are less bright, but still a kind of blue I've never seen anywhere else. Purple flecks in a turquoise pond.

I am carrying Bud Ripplemeyer's baby. He wants me to marry him before the baby is born. He wants to be able to say, Bud and Jane Ripplemeyer proudly announce . . .

He hooks his free hand around my neck and kisses me on the mouth, hard. "Marry me?" he says. I always hear a question mark these days, after everything he says.

Bud's not like Taylor—he's never asked me about India; it scares him. He wouldn't be interested in the forecast of an old fakir under a banyan tree. Bud was wounded in the war between my fate and my will. I think sometimes I saved his life by not marrying him.

I feel so potent, a goddess.

In the kitchen, today as on all Sundays, Mother Ripplemeyer is in charge. We have gone over to Mother's for our Sunday roast. Bud and his eight brothers and sisters were born in this house. From Baden, it's the first livable house on the second dirt road after you pass Madame Cleo's. Madame Cleo cuts and styles hair in a fuchsia pink geodesic dome.

When Bud and Karin's divorce became final, Karin got their fancy three-story brick house with the columns in front, their home for twenty-eight years. The house he bought after the divorce is low and squat, a series of add-ons. It had been a hired man's house. Eventually we'll take over Mother Ripplemeyer's house. Until then, we wait out here on three hundred acres, which isn't bad. My father raised nine of us on thirty acres.

This was a three-room frame house. He rents out the three hundred acres for hay. We added a new living room with an atrium when we moved in, and a small bedroom when we got word from the adoption agency in Des Moines that Du had made it out to Hong Kong. The house looks small and ugly from the dirt road, but every time I crunch into the driveway and park my old Rabbit between the rusting, abandoned machinery and the empty silo, the add-ons cozy me into thinking that all of us Ripplemeyers, even us new ones, belong.

Du is a Ripplemeyer. He was Du Thien. He was four-teen when we got him; now he's seventeen, a junior in high school. He does well, though he's sometimes con-temptuous. He barely spoke English when he arrived; now he's fluent, but with a permanent accent. "Like Kissinger," he says. They tell me I have no accent, but I don't sound Iowan, either. I'm like those voices on the telephone, very clear and soothing. Maybe Northern California, they say. Du says they're computer generated.

It was January when Du arrived at Des Moines from Honolulu with his agency escort. He was wearing an

ALOHA, Y'ALL T-shirt and a blue-jean jacket. We'd brought a new duffel coat with us, as instructed. Next to Bud, he seemed so tiny, so unmarked, for all he'd been through. The agency hadn't minded Bud's divorce. Karin could have made trouble but didn't. The agency was charmed by the notion of Bud's "Asian" wife, without inquiring too deeply. Du was one of the hard-to-place orphans.

He had never seen snow, never felt cold air, never worn a coat. We stopped at a McDonald's on the way back to Baden. When we parked, Du jumped down from the back, leaving the new coat on the seat. The wind chill was −35, and he waited for us in the middle of the parking lot in his ALOHA, Y'ALL T-shirt while we bundled up and locked the doors. He wasn't slapping his arms or blowing on his hands.

The day I came to Baden and walked into his bank with Mother Ripplemeyer, looking for a job, Bud was a tall, fit, fifty-year-old banker, husband of Karin, father of Buddy and Vern, both married farmers in nearby counties. Asia he'd thought of only as a soy-bean market. He'd gone to Beijing on a bankers' delegation and walked the Great Wall.

Six months later, Bud Ripplemeyer was a divorced man living with an Indian woman in a hired man's house five miles out of town. Asia had transformed him, made him reckless and emotional. He wanted to make up for fifty years of "selfishness," as he calls it. One night he saw a television special on boat people in Thai prisons, and he called the agency the next day. Fates are so intertwined in the modern world, how can a god keep them straight? A year after that, we had added Du to our life, and Bud was confined to a wheelchair.

Mother likes to cook, but she's crotchety this afternoon. It's one of her medium-bad days, which means she'll wink out on us entirely by the end. She is seventy-six, and sprightly in a Younkers pantsuit, white hair squeezed into curls by Madame Cleo, who trained in Ottumwa.

In Hasnapur a woman may be old at twenty-two.

I think of Vimla, a girl I envied because she lived in a two-story brick house with real windows. Our hut was mud. Her marriage was the fanciest the village had ever seen. Her father gave away a zippy red Maruti and a refrigerator in the dowry. When he was twenty-one her husband died of typhoid, and at twenty-two she doused herself with kerosene and flung herself on a stove, shouting to the god of death, "Yama, bring me to you."

The villagers say when a clay pitcher breaks, you see that the air inside it is the same as outside. Vimla set herself on fire because she had broken her pitcher; she saw there were no insides and outsides. We are just shells of the same Absolute. In Hasnapur, Vimla's isn't a sad story. The sad story would be a woman Mother Ripplemeyer's age still working on her shell, bothering to get her hair and nails done at Madame Cleo's.

*   *   *

Mother Ripplemeyer tells me her Depression stories. In the beginning, I thought we could trade some world-class poverty stories, but mine make her uncomfortable. Not that she's hostile. It's like looking at the name in my passport and seeing "Jyo—" at the beginning and deciding that her mouth was not destined to make those sounds. She can't begin to picture a village in Punjab. She doesn't mind my stories about New York and Florida because she's been to Florida many times and seen enough pictures of New York. I have to be careful about those stories. I have to be careful about nearly everything I say. If I talk about India, I talk about my parents.

I could tell her about water famines in Hasnapur, how at the dried-out well docile women turned savage for the last muddy bucketful. Even here, I store water in orange-juice jars, plastic milk bottles, tumblers, mixing bowls, any container I can find. I've been through thirsty times, and not that long ago. Mother doesn't think that's crazy. The Depression turned her into a hoarder, too. She's shown me her stock of tinfoil. She stashes the foil, neatly wrapped in a flannel sheet, in a drawer built into the bed for blankets and extra pillows.

She wonders, I know, why I left. I tell her, Education, which is true enough. She knows there is something else. I say, I had a mission. I want to protect her from too much reality.

She says she likes me better than she did Karin, though Karin grew up right here in Baden and Karin's mother, who is eighty-two, still picks her up for their Lutheran Mission

Relief Fund's quilting group. Last year the Relief Fund raised $18,000 for Ethiopia. Mother's group's quilt went for eleven hundred dollars to a bald, smiling man from Chicago who said it was for his granddaughter, but I read the commercial lettering on his panel truck.

Just before the divorce, according to Bud, Karin was agitating to stick Mother in the Lutheran Home. Mother senses I have different feelings about family.

The table is set and ready. Du's made a centerpiece out of some early flowers and I've polished the display rack of silver spoons. Bud has five brothers and three sisters, and they were all born or at least christened with silver spoons in their mouths. I, too, come from a family of nine. Figure the odds on that, Bud says. He has a brother in Minneapolis and a sister in Omaha and a brother named Vern Ripplemeyer, Jr., who died in Korea, the family's only other encounter with Asia. All the others are in Texas or California. After the divorce, Mother asked Karin to give the spoons back. "Call me an Indian giver," Mother likes to joke. "I mean *our* kind."

Du and Scott, whose father works down in the corn sweetener plant, are sprawled on the rug watching *Monster Truck Madness*. It's trucks versus tanks, and the tanks are creaming them. We bought ourselves a satellite dish the day after we first talked long distance to Du. There's no telling where this telecast is coming from.

Du's first question to Bud, in painful English over trans-

17

Pacific cable, was "You have television? You get?" He talked of having watched television in his home in Saigon. We got the point. He'd had two lives, one in Saigon and another in the refugee camp. In Saigon he'd lived in a house with a large family, and he'd been happy. He doesn't talk much about the refugee camp, other than that his mother cut hair, his older brother raised fighting fish, his married sister brought back live crabs and worms for him to eat whenever she could sneak a visit from her own camp. From a chatty agency worker we know that Du's mother and brother were hacked to death in the fields by a jealous madman, after they'd gotten their visas.

"Look at that sucker fly!" Scott shouts, crawling closer to the screen. "All right!" Mud scuds behind the Scarlet Slugger.

"Whoa, Nellie!" Du can match Scott shout for shout now. "Hold on, mama!" The Slugger is the body of a Chevy Blazer welded onto a World War II tank.

Mother wanders over to the television but doesn't sit down. In an instant replay we watch the Scarlet Slugger tear up the center of a bog. I can't help thinking, It looks like a bomb crater. Does Du even think such things? I don't know what he thinks. He's called Yogi in school, mainly because his name in English sounds more like "Yo." But he is a real yogi, always in control. I've told him my stories of India, the years between India and Iowa, hoping he'd share something with me. When they're over he usually says, "That's wild. Can I go now?"

"Holy Toledo!" Mother is into it.

"Mom, it's okay, isn't it, if Scott stays for dinner?"

"If it's okay with his parents."

Scott grins at me with his perfect teeth. I envy him his teeth. We had no dentist in Hasnapur. For a long time we had no doctor either, except for Vaccinations-sahib, who rode in and out of the village in a WHO jeep. My teeth look as though they've been through slugfests. Du's seventeen and wears braces. Orthodontics was the Christmas present he asked for.

"And if the two of you wash the beans," I add.

"You aren't making the yellow stuff, Mrs. R.?" I detect disappointment.

"I will if you name it."

I see him whispering to Du, and Du's bony shoulder shrug. "Globey?" he says.

It's close enough. I took gobi aloo to the Lutheran Relief Fund craft fair last week. I am subverting the taste buds of Elsa County. I put some of last night's matar panir in the microwave. It goes well with pork, believe me.

Bud wheels himself in from his study. "I can't let the kid do it!" The kid is Darrel, whose financial forms he's been studying. "It's plain stupid. Gene would never forgive me."

I've sent away for the latest in wheelchairs, automated and really maneuverable. The doctor said, "I had a patient once who had his slugs pierced and hung on a chain around his neck." Bud said to throw them out. He didn't want to see how flattened they'd got, bouncing off his bones. The doctor is from Montana. I haven't been west of Lincoln, Nebraska. Every night the frontier creeps a little closer.

Think of banking as your business, I want to tell Bud. Don't make moral decisions for Darrel. It's his farm now. He can make half a million by selling, buy his franchise and a house, and I can look out on a golf course, which won't kill me. Bud gets too involved. It almost killed him two years ago.

"Watch him, Dad!" Du whoops. "Watch him take off!"

Bud puts away the Financial Statement and Supporting Schedules form he's been penciling. He skids and wheels closer to Du to watch the Python.

"Can you do a wheelie yet, Mr. R.?" Scott jokes.

"Boy!" He smiles. "That thing gives the guy great air!"

The Python's built himself a fancy floating suspension. Father and son watch the Snakeman win his class.

On the screen Cut Tire Class vehicles, frail as gnats, skim over churned-up mud. Helmeted men give me victory signs. They all plan on winning tonight. Nitro Express, Brawling Babe, Insane Expectations. Move over, I whisper.

Over the bleached grounds of Baden, Iowa, loose, lumpy rainclouds are massing. Good times, best times, are coming. Move over.

Mother paces between the windows. "Poor Vern." Her hands pick at lint balls I can't see. "It's blowing so hard he'll never find his way back from the barn. A man can die in a storm like this."

Bud flashes anxiety at me. His father was Vern. I calm him with a touch. He rests his head on my hip. "Kiss an old fool for love?" He grins. I bring my face down close to his big face. He kisses my chin, my cheeks, my eyelids, my temples. His lips scuttle across my forehead; they warm the cold pale star of my scar. My third eye glows, a spotlight trained on lives to come. This isn't a vision to share with Bud. He is happy. And I am happy enough.

The lemon-pale afternoon swirls indoors through torn window screens. The first lightning bugs of summer sparkle. I feel the tug of opposing forces. Hope and pain. Pain and hope.

Mother moves around the room, turning on lamps. "Seen the quilt?" she says. "How much do you think it'll bring? Thirty-five? Forty?"

In the white lamplight, ghosts float toward me. Jane, Jasmine, Jyoti.

"It'll depend on the Christian conscience of strangers," Bud jokes. "You might get more than thirty-five."

"Think how many people thirty-five dollars will feed out there."

Out there. I am not sure what Mother imagines. On the edge of the world, in flaming deserts, mangled jungles, squelchy swamps, missionaries save the needy. Out There, the darkness. But for me, for Du, In Here, safety. At least for now.

Oh, the wonder! the wonder!

21

3

DARREL was looking a little out of control in the Hy-Vee parking lot last week. He was trying to avoid me, but I didn't read the signs in time. I called out his name and started running. He was carrying a case of Heileman's Old Style and a six-pack of blue Charmin. He'd nearly stashed it all in the front seat by the time I got there. His eyes were red and unfocused and he was unsteady on his feet.

Bud always says, of young farmers or the middle-aged ones with shaky operations, Look out for drinking. I don't know if Darrel's a drinker. I do not count off-hours drunkenness a sin. I invited him for dinner that night, but he politely refused. That is, it started politely, with a decent enough excuse, but then he saw me watching him and he knew there was no good excuse except that he was drunk and intending to stay that way.

Since his father died, Darrel's had no time for fun. No dates, no movies, no vacation weekends. In the spring, that's understandable, but not the winter. Iowa farmers pamper themselves in the winter if they can afford it. Gene and Carol always did. The blond girl who visited for a while didn't seem too helpful. We had her over with Darrel. She was sullen, cut out for nobler ventures. "It's the hogs" is his usual excuse, "you have to *baby-sit* hogs." He has a hundred and fifty Hampshires; Gene had wanted to build up to three hundred.

Bud says, "It takes a good man to raise hogs." Gene was a good man. Bud's talking discipline, strength, patience, character. Husbandry. All of that is in short supply. Maybe Darrel doesn't have it, in which case a golf course isn't a betrayal. Most people in Elsa County have lost it. Just look at all the dents and unpainted rust spots on the cars in front of the Hy-Vee.

"I couldn't go another round with Bud," Darrel finally admitted.

"He's just trying to make you see both sides, that's all."

"Jane, his mind is closed against me. He's just dead set against non-ag uses for anyone's ground, especially Gene Lutz's ground. But then he turns around and won't lend me enough to get my crops in and still expand my herd. He thinks he's my goddamn father."

I felt awful for him, and worse for myself. I didn't want to be disloyal. But what he said is true. The First Bank of

Baden has survived in harsh times because Bud can read people's characters. Out here, it's character that pays the bills or doesn't, because everything else is just about equal.

"Bud's trying to tie my hands and pin my ears back. He thinks I'm a lousy manager. He thinks he has all the answers. Well, tell him something from me, tell him to bring me rain if he's God." Then, almost immediately, he said, "I'm sorry. I've been drinking. I apologize."

We're dry right now. The rains will come. "Let me drive you home," I say.

He lets himself be led, fumbling with his beer and toilet paper, to my Rabbit. He's drunker than I thought. He drums his fingers on the case of beer. He's like my brothers, with their scooter repair. They work and drink. It's the only life they know, and I wouldn't call them flawed.

All alone he's backhoed a 40,000-gallon pit for his hogs' nightsoil, and with sewer men and electricians on the weekends, he's built a self-sufficient city for hogs. Once the pump is working, they'll fertilize two hundred acres automatically, organically, and perpetually. A farmer's dream. I've told Bud that financing this project is his best hostage against the golfing boys from Dalton. No farmer could walk away from it. But he thinks it's too big for Darrel.

Darrel's right about the bottom line. Bud doesn't trust him.

Most nights, when Bud and I head to the Dairy Queen after supper, we can see Darrel up on the crossbeams of his hog pen. It's already bigger than Gene's old barn, and a lot more secure. Last week when I drove him home down his

access lane between the rows of maple and elder, he so-
bered up as he just stared at the roof skeleton rising high
above the poured-concrete floor and the metal sidings. The
sheer scale of his achievement! You could smell the hogs
and hear their squealing. That unfinished building looked
like a landbound Ark. Big sloppy Shadow came out to
greet him.

He was slow, more reluctant than drunk, in getting out.
"I'd like to invite you in someday," he says. *In* seems to be
saying something different from *over.* More exclusive. "I've
been practicing with some of your recipes. Need an expert
to tell me how I'm doing."

4

Bud calls me Jane. Me Bud, you Jane. I didn't get it at first. He kids. Calamity Jane. Jane as in Jane Russell, not Jane as in Plain Jane. But Plain Jane is all I want to be. Plain Jane is a role, like any other. My genuine foreignness frightens him. I don't hold that against him. It frightens me, too.

In Baden, I am Jane. Almost.

Last week on our favorite cable channel, Du and I saw twenty INS agents raid a lawn furniture factory in Texas. The man in charge of the raid called it a factory, but all it was was a windowless shed the size of a two-car garage. We got to hear agents whisper into walkie-talkies, break down a door, kick walls for hollowed-out hiding places. They were very thorough.

Du snickered, but he gives no sign of caring, one side or the other. He's very careful that way. There were only two Mexicans in the shed. They ducked behind a chaise longue that was only half-webbed. One minute they were squatting on the floor webbing lawn furniture at some insane wage—I know, I've been there—and the next they were spread-eagled on the floor. The camera caught one Mexican throwing up. The INS fellow wouldn't uncuff him long enough for him to wipe the muck off his face.

I thought I heard Du mutter, "Asshole." And I realized I didn't know who were the assholes, the cowboys or the Indians.

A woman in a flowered dress said, "I don't think they're bad people, you know. It's just that there's too many of them. Yesterday I opened the front door to get the morning papers and there were three of them using my yard as their personal toilet."

The reporter, a thin, tense man with razor burns, stopped a woman in an Olds. "To tell you the truth," she said, "I don't know what to feel anymore." The reporter got ready to move off to somebody else, but she stopped him. "Steve, my husband, lost his job. That was last November. We were doing so good, now we can't make the house and car payments. Are you listening, Mr. President?"

I wanted to shout to the lady, Mrs. Steve, Two years ago Bud got shot and will never walk again. Are *you* listening? What kind of crazy connection are you trying to make between Mexicans and car payments? Who's the victim here? And what about Du? Mr. President, what about Du?

The officer in charge flat-handed the mike away, but I

thought I heard, "The border's like Swiss cheese and all the mice are squirming through the holes."

So they got two. Which meant that there had to be scores more who scampered away at the start of the raid. Du and me, we're the ones who didn't get caught. The only mystery is who'll get caught and who'll escape. Du made it out of the refugee camp, and his brother didn't.

I visit Du in his room. He's sitting over his typewriter. I smell tobacco, nothing more serious. A mother, even one no older than a sister, can be forgiven if she looks in because the door is open a crack, because it gives a little when she leans her shoulder on it.

"Try me with your homework? I used to be pretty good in my day."

He laughs, but something is wrong. I can see it in the stiffened neck. "Thanks, but I don't think you know much about Teddy Roosevelt." He gives his history book, jacketed in brown paper as demanded by Mr. Skola, an irritated shove. "Speak softly but carry a big stick. I bet that's all you know about Teddy Roosevelt."

Truth is, I didn't know that. I know a little bit about one of the Roosevelts, and about his wife, who was a friend of Indian freedom. At least, Masterji said she was.

At the last PTA meeting Mr. Skola sought me out by the coffee urn and said, "Yogi's in a hurry to become all-American, isn't he?" I said, "Yes. He doesn't carry a dictionary around anymore." And then he said, "He's a quick study, isn't he? They were like that, the kids who hung around us in Saigon." He didn't make "quick study" sound like anything you'd like to be. We're all quick studies, I should have said. Once we start letting go—let go just one thing, like not wearing our normal clothes, or a turban or not wearing a tika on the forehead—the rest goes on its own down a sinkhole. When he first arrived, Du kept a small shrine in his room, with pictures, a candle, and some dried fragrances. I don't know when he gave it up.

"I tried a little Vietnamese on him," Mr. Skola went on, "and he just froze up."

I suppressed my shock, my disgust. This country has so many ways of humiliating, of disappointing. How *dare* you? What must he have thought? His history teacher in Baden, Iowa, just happens to know a little street Vietnamese? Now where would he have picked it up? There are no harmless, compassionate ways to remake oneself. We murder who we were so we can rebirth ourselves in the images of dreams. All this I should have explained to the red-faced, green-shirted, yellow-tied Mr. Skola. Instead, I said, "Du's first few weeks with us, my husband thought we had an autistic child on our hands!"

I apologize to Du. "I won't bug you anymore, then. You've got your Big Stick to learn up. I'll leave you alone."

"Before you go . . ." he calls to me. He hunts for something in the top left-hand drawer of his desk. It is a drawer he keeps locked with a mechanism he improvised out of tossed-out farm equipment. He's an inventor, a little like Prakash, exceptional and impatient. We're getting him a computer this summer, and sending him to Iowa City for college-credit training.

"I got something for you."

He's a magpie, or a fence. Soon he won't be able to close that drawer. He's a materialist, no question, and his room is a warehouse. He's hoarded things, big things like road signs and Drug Town posters, medium things like record players and radios thrown out even by Goodwill, and little things like nail files. What he owns seems to matter to him less than owning itself. He needs to own. Owning is rebellion, it means not sharing, it means survival. He ate bugs and worms and rodents. He lived. He's a quick study, all right.

A rhinestone ladybug winks in Du's cupped palm. "Du!" I stare at the ridged and calloused skin welted by thick brown fate lines. "They look like diamonds!"

"What if they were?"

He pins the ladybug on my shirt. For a moment his face glows and I think he will kiss me. "You were meant to have pretty things," he says.

Secrets roll like barbed wire between us. I don't ask where he bought or found the pin that glints on my Madras shirt. But as I lie awake this night, the first night that gives signs of not cooling down, Du joins the ghosts of men. He is a phantom lover, he watches me; perhaps he has been watching every night, in his secret, inventive ways.

5

TWO days ago I was sitting in the Gynecology Annex of the University Hospital down in Iowa City waiting for Dr. Mrs. Jaswani to get off the phone and call me in, when the woman next to me on the sofa started sobbing into a book she held pressed tight to her face. There was a man's picture on the back of the book, just about the right size for the woman's head; I almost laughed out loud. I couldn't tell her age because of the book, but she looked fitly scrawny in sweat pants. Frizzy gray hair spewed out on either side of the dust jacket, not that gray hair meant that she had come to see Dr. Kwang in Infertility instead of Dr. Jaswani. The University Hospital's gotten into infertility and gerontology in a biggish way. I know this from Bud, because he's processed home mortgages for three of the Infertility guys and they've all bought properties for over two hundred thousand.

Kwang, Liu, Patel, I've met them all. Poke around in a major medical facility and suddenly you're back in Asia, which I find very reassuring. I trust only Asian doctors, Asian professionals. What we've gone through must count for something. "It's going to be all right," I said to the woman with the book over her face. "Can I get you some coffee?"

We were the only two people in the waiting room. I could hear the nurse but I couldn't see her. She was reporting on somebody's endometrial biopsy results in her broad booming voice. The girl at the reception desk was scrolling information on her computer screen. She had her Walkman on, anyway.

"Thanks, no," the woman said. She had a striking face, all sharp angles. Crying didn't puff it up. "Caffeine and I aren't friends."

"I'll get some water, then," I said.

"I don't know what happened," the woman said. "One minute I was thinking about the Ricky doll I used to love to death and the next minute I'm this wreck."

"I'm so sorry." I got her water from the fountain. The Dixie cup was tiny to begin with, and even the water it held I managed to slosh on the way. These mornings my fingers feel quite swollen.

She shrugged her thanks. The sip she took was out of politeness. "You probably don't know what a Ricky doll is."

She must have been an older student, or a professor. Educated people are interested in differences; they assume that I'm different from them but exempted from being one of "them," the knife-wielding undocumenteds hiding in basements webbing furniture.

In Baden, the farmers are afraid to suggest I'm different. They've seen the aerograms I receive, the strange lettering I can decipher. To them, alien knowledge means intelligence. They want to make me familiar. In a pinch, they'll admit that I might look a little different, that I'm a "dark-haired girl" in a naturally blond county. I have a "darkish complexion" (in India, I'm "wheatish"), as though I might be Greek from one grandparent. I'm from a generic place, "over there," which might be Ireland, France, or Italy. I'm not a Lutheran, which isn't to say I might not be Presbyterian. About which they're ignorant; farmers are famously silent, and not ashamed.

Taylor's friends in New York used to look at me and say, "You're Iranian, right?" If I said no, then, "Pakistani, Afghan, or Punjabi?" They were strikingly accurate about most things, and always out to improve themselves. Even though I was just an *au pair*, professors would ask if I could help them with Sanskrit or Arabic, Devanagari or Gurumukhi script. I can read Urdu, not Arabic. I can't read Sanskrit. They had things they wanted me to translate, paintings they wanted me to decipher. They were very democratic that way. For them, experience leads to knowledge, or else it is wasted. For me, experience must be forgotten, or else it will kill.

But the other girls in the building, the other day

mummies—sorry, "caregivers"—who descended on the lobby at eight o'clock every morning, down from Harlem or over from Brooklyn, and took over the children while the mothers went out to teach or study or edit or just do what they do, assumed only that I was from "the islands," like they were. That was democratic, too.

They assumed I had a past, like them, about which I didn't tell too much. Most of them had children back in Jamaica or Trinidad or Santo Domingo. They assumed I did, too. I didn't have a child, but I had a past that I was still fleeing. Perhaps still am.

"Little Ricky Ricardo," she said. She squeaked her nails up and down the spine of the book. I could tell she was hurting. "It can't mean much to you."

"You'll be okay."

"So I waited too long," she said. "I wrote poems. I was going to be the next Adrienne Rich. I mean, it isn't the end of the world or anything."

She got me there, too.

"You have nice hips," she said. But she gave the "you" a generic sweep. You teeming millions with wide hips breeding like roaches on wide-hipped continents. "Wide. Nature meant you to carry babies."

"Thank you," I said. What else could I have said?

"You're pregnant, aren't you?" I didn't deny it. "It was easy, wasn't it? You didn't wait, you're lucky."

The truth is, I am young enough to bear children into the next century. But. I feel old, very old, millennia old, a bug-eyed viewer of beginnings and ends. In the old Hindu books they say that in the eye of the creator, mountains rise and fall like waves on the ocean.

It wasn't hard to get pregnant, but it wasn't very natural, either. It shames Bud that now, for sex, I must do all the work, all the moving, that I will always be on top. I will do this. But for having this baby, I required Dick Kwang's assistance. Bud was very nervous, made jokes about "Dick and Jane" that Dong-jin Kwang and I didn't understand. Bud said he'd watched the inseminators do their job a thousand times, but he never thought he'd be so intimately involved.

It was Mother who got us together. Professionally. The first time she met me, she asked if I was good with numbers. Passably, I said. She assumed I was a student at the university; I didn't disabuse her.

"My son is always looking for smart, reliable tellers. Let's take a trip over there." She thought we'd hit it off. The hours were flexible, good for a student. I took her up on it.

He came running out of the office that day. "Mother! Who have you brought us, a maharani? I hope you haven't eaten, Your Highness, because I'm just headed out the door."

☆　☆　☆

"Oh, God, I love you so much," he says. "I have never seen anyone so beautiful." He doesn't often make these pronouncements, they are part of his abject position, his helplessness. We are back home from Mother Ripplemeyer's. Du in the living room watching television, Bud and I are in the bedroom. Bud may no longer be a whole man, but desire hasn't deserted him. Lust deprived of spontaneous fulfillment: that's what shames him now. Once he had been in control; once he had been an impulsive pursuer.

After I prepare him for bed, undo the shoes, pull off the pants, sponge-bathe him, he likes me to change roles, from caregiver to temptress, and I try to do it convincingly, walking differently, frowning, smiling . . . I take off my Sunday clothes very carefully in the bathroom, with the door open, the light on. I am to linger there, and act as though I am alone. I brush my teeth, a long, long time; I rub myself against the lavatory's edge. When we first met and began making love in my rented room and in the motel rooms of neighboring towns, he was active and inventive, very sure of himself, he loved games. Now I must do all the playing, provide the surprises. I don't mind. His upper body is enormously strong, the bench press of love. It isn't the preparations (for all their awkwardness and crudeness) that I rage against. What kills me in this half-lit bedroom is the look of torture, excitement, desperation on Bud's face as he watches me.

Desire can end only one way, tonight or any other night. I come to bed, crawling over the covers, until a pair of immensely strong, blond-haired arms enfold me. He can lift me, even from his prone position, lift me and center me and keep me in the air till I feel his arms trembling, and as my legs, my breasts, my face dip to touch his chest, I can feel the ripple of his heart; our flesh makes loud slapping noises. Then it is my turn to take charge. There are massages I must administer, pushing him on the prostate, tools I must push up him so that, at least on very special nights, he can ejaculate.

Bud's eyes are closed, face contorted. "Sweet Jane," he mutters. "I've brought you to this. The old big beads trick."

I hush him with my lips. I do not know the pain he suffers, if any, if bliss lies this close to agony, if he is on a different plane. When love collapses, I let myself fall to his chest and his heart is like a fist beating me wherever we touch.

Tonight, as Bud's breath shivers back to normal and the hard thumping of his heart softens to a beat, I can almost follow, a sliver of blue television light exposes two small pools of darkness at the base of our bedroom door. Our bedroom door is open, just a crack. The shadow pools gather into one, and disappear. A line of blue light edges our door, then snaps off.

A few seconds later we hear, "Night, Mom and Dad." He moves so quietly.

It is still spring, hot days, cool nights, Iowa's gentlest month. Bud is already in the first flutterings of sleep. The house is dark, full of unacted drama. Lying awake, trying to regulate my breathing with my heart, with Bud's light snore, trying to put my head back on the pillow, I watch the patterns on the ceiling, framed photos on the dresser, my lover falling through layers of private pain. I get up, briefly, and move his wheelchair back to the corner, and fold it. On nights like this, with a full moon beating down like an auxiliary sun, the farmers say you can practically hear the corn and beans ripping their way through the ground. This night I feel torn open like the hot dry soil, parched.

6

In a makeshift birthing hut in Hasnapur, Jullundhar District, Punjab, India, I was born the year the harvest was so good that even my father, the reluctant tiller of thirty acres, had grain to hoard for drought. If I had been a boy, my birth in a bountiful year would have marked me as lucky, a child with a special destiny to fulfill. But daughters were curses. A daughter had to be married off before she could enter heaven, and dowries beggared families for generations. Gods with infinite memories visited girl children on women who needed to be punished for sins committed in other incarnations.

My mother's past must have been heavy with wrongs. I was the fifth daughter, the seventh of nine children.

When the midwife carried me out, my sisters tell me, I had a ruby-red choker of bruise around my throat and sapphire fingerprints on my collarbone.

When I revealed this to Taylor's wife, Wylie—I was their undocumented "caregiver" during my years in Manhattan—she missed the point and shrieked at my "foremothers." Listening to Wylie I thought I understood the philosophy behind Agent Orange. Wylie would over-kill. My mother was a sniper. She wanted to spare me the pain of a dowryless bride. My mother wanted a happy life for me.

I survived the sniping. My grandmother may have named me Jyoti, Light, but in surviving I was already Jane, a fighter and adapter.

God's cruel, my mother complained, to waste brains on a girl. And God's still more cruel, she said, to make a fifth daughter beautiful instead of the first. By the time my turn to marry came around, there would be no dowry money left to gift me the groom I deserved. I was seven then, a reader, a counter, a picture drawer to whom Masterji, the oldest and sourest teacher in our school (B.A. Patiala, failed), lent his own books. I was a whiz in Punjabi and Urdu, and the first likely female candidate for English instruction he'd ever had. He had a pile of English books, some from the British Council Library, some with USIS stickers. I remember a thin one, *Shane*, about an American village much like Punjab, and *Alice in Wonderland*, which gave me nightmares. The British books were thick, with more long words per page. I remember *Great Expectations* and *Jane Eyre*, both of which I was forced to abandon because they were too difficult.

God is cruel to partition the country, she said, to uproot our family from a city like Lahore where we had lived for centuries, and fling us to a village of flaky mud huts. In Lahore my parents had lived in a big stucco house with porticoes and gardens. They had owned farmlands, shops. An alley had been named after a great-uncle. In our family lore Lahore was magic and Lahore was chaos.

Mataji, my mother, couldn't forget the Partition Riots. Muslims sacked our house. Neighbors' servants tugged off earrings and bangles, defiled grottoes, sabered my grandfather's horse. Life shouldn't have turned out that way! I've never been to Lahore, but the loss survives in the instant replay of family story: forever Lahore smokes, forever my parents flee.

Nothing is fair. God is cruel. Now I hear these words as love's refrain. Mataji loved me fiercely. Love made her panic at what was in store. All over our district, bad luck dogged dowryless wives, rebellious wives, barren wives. They fell into wells, they got run over by trains, they burned to death heating milk on kerosene stoves. She scolded my father into letting me stay in school after classes were over and daze myself with Masterji's hoard of English-language books.

*　*　*

My father was a man who had given up long before I was born. People said of him that he looked like a Lahori landlord; refined, delicate of feature. He maintained authority even while lacking a position. I have his looks. Except when it was absolutely necessary to plant or to harvest, he would lie on a charpoy under a flowering jasmine tree all day. Even without money he dressed well, in what he insisted were the last of his old Lahore kurtas.

He would tune in to the Pakistani radio broadcasts from Lahore, and listen for their Punjabi-language shows. The names of those singers and actors from the Pakistan side were more familiar to me, growing up, than their Indian counterparts. Otherwise, he detested Urdu and Muslims, which he naturally associated with the loss of our fortune. He refused to speak Hindi as well, considering it the language of Gandhi, the man who had approved the partition of Punjab and the slaughter of millions. After fleeing Lahore, Pitaji had been cast adrift in an uncaring, tasteless, corrupt, coarse, ignorant world.

"These Bombay mangoes would choke a goat!" he'd say when I brought him the Alphonsos I'd haggled smartly for in the bazaar. He said the Punjabi you heard a beggar mutter by the trash pits of Lahore was poetry compared to the crow-talk Punjabi of the richest merchants in Jullundhar and Hasnapur. "You should have heard those Lahori barristers and politicians give speeches. Their words had wings." Lahore visionaries, Lahore women, Lahore music, Lahore ghazals: my father lived in a bunker.

Fact is, there was a difference. My father was right to notice it and to let it set a standard. But that pitcher is broken. It is the same air this side as that. He'll never see Lahore again and I never have. Only a fool would let it rule his life.

7

I WAS born eighteen years after the Partition Riots. My whole world was the village of Hasnapur. It wasn't a dead-end corner of a flat, baked, violent land at all. I remember sneaking into my friend Vimla's house and clicking the light switch on-off/on-off when electricity came to the brick houses of the rich traders-down the road. My brothers hated Vimla's father; they called him Potatoes-babu behind his back, but I didn't care. The naked light bulb swaying at the end of a braided cord was magic! With my palm on the light switch, I felt totally in control.

In our house we had to finish eating, cleaning up, sewing, reading, before nightfall. Oil for clay lamps was expensive and not always available. Ghosts and spirits took over in the dark. If you had electricity, you could drive out even the most tenacious spirit. When electricity came to Hasnapur and more and more people got it, at least enough for a light, my mother complained that now all the ghosts in the big houses would be chased to the ring of unlighted huts—ours, and the Mazbis' even farther out—where they could hide and cause mischief.

I remember when the hand pump was put up by a government man, and we didn't have to trudge with our full pitchers all the way from the well or from the riverbank. In the doctor's storefront clinic I saw my first television picture. The doctor was a tall, mustached man, and he showed stern how-to videos about the efficacies of small families and clean hands. I had the scrubbed-rawest hands. I boiled the river water three and four times, when everyone else just let the mud settle before drinking.

One time we saw a real film. It was in school and it was American. Masterji loved things American. He had a nephew in California. He read us his letters. Farmers there were like we were; they, too, worried about weather, about families sticking together during terrible times, about arranging decent weddings for their children. He said the world would be a saner planet if it were run by farmers instead of by generals and politicians. The movie was dubbed in Hindi and had a lot of singing and dancing. It was called Seven Village Girls Find Seven Boys to Marry, or something like that, but the songs weren't as good as our Bombay ones.

Mataji bullied Pitaji into letting me stay in school six years, which was three years longer than my sisters. They had been found cut-rate husbands by one of Pitaji's

Amritsar cousins. The cousin, a large dogmatic woman, said that big-city men prefer us village girls because we are brought up to be caring and have no minds of our own. Village girls are like cattle; whichever way you lead them, that is the way they will go.

My two brothers, Arvind-prar and Hari-prar, had taken themselves off to the town of Jullundhar, hoping they could get into a diploma program in some technical school. Their plan was to find jobs in a Gulf emirate—we had cousins who called themselves electrical engineers and were sending lakhs of rupees back from Qatar and Bahrain. They were fixers and tinkerers, not students. Without going to a fancy institute of technology my brothers were able to repair our storefront clinic's television set. (Potatoes-babu had sent his son to a fancy institute in Loughborough, England, where he ended up marrying an English girl and not coming back, even for Vimla's death.) Hari-prar and Arvind-prar joked that when the time came they'd smuggle me into the examination hall so I could write their exams. They were proud of me because Masterji said I wrote the best English compositions, and they had me translate instruction manuals and write school or job applications.

From his charpoy in the courtyard, Pitaji protested in soft grunts. "That Masterji fellow thinks you are a lotus blooming in cow dung?" or "Get firewood! Boil tea! Feed the chickens!" Mataji and I humored him because the mustached doctor had told us he had hypertension. I stayed in school.

The work at home didn't slow me down. I *liked* doing chores. At dawn I pushed our Mazbi maidservant aside and boiled the milk myself—four times—because the maid had no clue to cleanliness and pasteurization. Just before dusk, the best hour for marketing, since vegetable vendors discounted what they hadn't sold and what they couldn't keep overnight, I'd go with neighborhood women and get my mother the best bargains. The women liked having me with them because I could add fast in my head, and because I always caught the lime and chillies vendor when he cheated them. In return, the crabbiest of the women taught me how to haggle prices down. She was a widow, and for herself she bought only half kilos of potatoes and onions (as a widow she should not have eaten onions); I knew even then I was witnessing permissible rebellion.

Dida, Pitaji's mother, was the only one in the family to make a fuss about my staying on in school, but she spent most months of the year in an ashram in the holy city of Hardwar and didn't torment us with visits too often. Her line was "You're going to have to wear out your sandals getting rid of this one." She spoke only to Pitaji. Sometimes she changed to "Some women think they own the world because their husbands are too lazy to beat them," but Mataji just went about her cooking with her mouth zipped and her veiled head down.

The crisis came when Dida announced that she, through a pious and ailing woman living in the same

47

ashram, had finally located a passable groom willing to take me off their hands. I wasn't quite thirteen then. The woman's sister (Dida thought the sister lived in Ludhiana, but she would check it out) had a neighbor who owned almost two hundred acres of well-irrigated ground. The farmer was known to have four sons, one of whom was a widower with three children and needed a new wife to look after them.

Mataji and Dida could have been Sivaji and Aurangzeb out of Masterji's book on Indian history. Their battle was fierce and wordless. The neighborhood sided with Dida on this one. The widower's father was a rich man, and Mataji was a bitter woman with a mangled mind to hold up my chance at a comfortable life. Who did I think I was to turn down a once-in-a-lifetime bridegroom?

Masterji must have heard that he was likely to lose me to the Ludhiana widower. He biked all the way to our adobe compound one Sunday morning, his white beard rolled spiffily tight and his long hair tucked under a crisp char-treuse turban, to confront my father, the Lahori Hindu gentleman. He was even carrying a kirpan, which meant that for him this was a special occasion. Masterji was a Sikh. All Sikh men in our village, even the low-caste converted Mazbis, and quite a few of the older men, kept their hair and beards, but very few went around with their ceremonial daggers strapped to their chests all day long.

In school we Hindu girls had thought of Masterji as a

religious man, a pious Sikh, but very noncommunal, until pamphlets accusing him of being a bad Sikh—of smoking, for instance—started showing up in classrooms. At the time we assumed the posters were a prank. There was a new Sikh boys' gang, the Khalsa Lions, who liked action. Khalsa means pure. As Lions of Purity, the gang dressed in white shirts and pajamas and indigo turbans, and all of them toted heavy kirpans on bandoliers. They had money to zigzag through the bazaar on scooters, but since they were, like Arvind-prar and Hari-prar, farmers' sons, we assumed the money for scooters came from smuggling liquor and guns in and out of Pakistan. In villages close enough to the border, smuggling was not an unacceptable profession.

When Masterji unstraddled his bike, we noticed the damp red stain on the back of his turban. Tomato seeds still stuck to the stain. The Khalsa Lions had taken to hurling fruit and stones from their scooters.

The maidservant dragged the only chair we had—an old wooden one missing a slat—to where Pitaji and Dida were arguing, and went off to boil sweet milky tea for the men. Mataji and I stayed inside, out of sight, within hearing range.

We heard Pitaji say, "Hooligans! Now they're throwing sticks and stones; next month they'll throw bombs!"

"Good," Mataji whispered. "They're speaking in English. Dida will be less of a problem."

Masterji had his game plan. "It isn't like Lahore, is it? Lahore was Rome. But as we know from the great historian

49

Mr. Gibbon, where there is a rising there is also a falling. Hooligans who soar must also come down."

My father, softened by the analogy, sighed. "We should have had our Nero to fiddle while we burned." Masterji was also Lahori, where even the Sikhs, according to my father, were men of culture. Then he short-cut the preliminaries. "Masterji, you are here to tell me that there is a lotus blooming in the middle of all this filth, no?"

In Hasnapur the metaphorical and the literal converge. On the far side of the courtyard, by the buffalo enclosure, the maidservant's pretty little girl was scooping up fresh dung, kneading it thick with straw chips, and patting them into cakes the size of her palms. She would slap the cakes down on the adobe walls of our kitchen enclosure and leave them to dry into fuel.

Masterji kept his eyes on the little girl working the buffalo dung. "An educator's duty, sir, is not to burn the flower with the dung."

"In this country"—Pitaji laughed—"we are having too many humans and not enough buffaloes."

"Yes, yes," Masterji agreed, too quickly, "in hot-weather countries Mother Nature is too fecund. That is why it is important that modern ladies go for secondary-school education and find themselves positions. They are not shackling themselves to wifehood and maternity first chance. Surely you know, sir, that in our modern society many bright ladies are finding positions?"

"Positions?" Pitaji demanded. "What do you mean, precisely? A lady working for strange men? Money changing hands?"

Pitaji's face caricatured outrage. I thought for a minute that a tea stain would darken Masterji's chartreuse turban.

"I am a reasonable man," Pitaji said. "We are modern people. We let the girl decide." Then he called to me to come. I ran. He held both my hands. "Masterji wants you to go to more school." He loosened his grip, giving me the chance to break away. I stayed. He went on: "Masterji is wanting you to work in a bank. You can be steno. You have my blessing. He is wanting you to learn more English and also shorthand. You are wanting position of steno in the State Bank?"

"No," I said. "I don't want to be a steno. I don't want to be a teller, either."

My father looked stunned. He coddled my rough, scratched hands. He turned to Masterji, an ecstatic man. "You have heard it straight from the filly's mouth, as it were, isn't it? The girl refuses further education. The thing is that bright ladies are bearing bright sons, that is nature's design."

I didn't pull my hands out of Pitaji's palms as I said, "I want to be a doctor and set up my own clinic in a big town." Like the mustached doctor in the bazaar clinic, I wanted to scrape off cataracts, fit plastic legs on stumps, work miracles.

My father gasped. "The girl is mad! I'll write in the back of the dictionary: The girl is mad!"

Dida caught on for the first time. She said in Punjabi, "Blame the mother. Insanity has to come from somewhere. It's the mother who is mad."

All that day and deep into the night, we heard their

chorus. "The girl is mad. Her mother is mad. The whole country is mad. Kali Yuga has already come."

And deeper into that night I heard the thwock of blows.

But in the morning Mataji said, "They've come around. Just make sure you ace your exams." She smiled. She smiled so wide that the fresh split in her upper lip opened up and started bleeding again. When I said to Wylie once that my mother loved me so much she tried to kill me, or she would have killed herself, she pulled Duff, their daughter, a little closer to her.

8

ONLY the brick houses of rich traders like Potatoes-babu had toilets put up in courtyards. They were tiny thatch-walled privies on stilts. You squatted above a hole and heard the waste plop many feet below into a huge earthenware bowl full of lye. The walls crawled with roaches and spiders. At Vimla's you could smell the lye from every room. I much preferred going to the fields with the neighborhood women. We went early, in pre-dawn dark, before the men woke, so they couldn't spy on us. My mother never came with us. She was a modest and superior Lahori woman, so modest and superior that as a child I'd assumed her body was free of daily functions. For the neighborhood women, though, the latrine hour was the most companionable time. They squatted in a row and gossiped. I liked to listen.

Three days after Masterji's visit I trekked as usual with my favorite group along the banks of a nullah. Almost all of them were married, and listening to their jokes made me feel very adult. The pale sky hung low over paler eucalyptus. The wheat fields were parrot green and fenced in with brambly black branches of acacia. The clover patches could have been scatter rugs.

Our route cut across a treed lot where the Khalsa Lions hung out, hacking branches thick as staffs to beat people and knock them off their bikes and scooters. Sometimes they'd cut down whole trees and drag them across the only road, forcing motor traffic to stop. Then they'd threaten the passengers, sometimes robbing them. The good thing about the Khalsa Lions using that lot was that I could stop back afterward and gather up firewood from their discards. That day I found the biggest staff ever, stuck in a wreath of thorny brush. I had to crawl on cold stony ground, and of course thorns bloodied my arms, but the moment my fist closed over the head of the staff, I felt a buzz of power.

By the time I got to the fields, the adults were already squatting. Their brass pitchers of wash-up water gleamed in the dawn light. Spilled water crusted into ice wafers. I waited till my favorite bush was deserted, and watched two paunchy, jovial women tickle each other's bulbous behinds with leafy sprigs and grass. This was the "Ladies' Hour." Sober women became crude, lusty, raucous.

"Oh, snake, snake, I see a snake!"

"You saw a very skinny little snake last night. Arré, you woke up the same snake in my house!"

We knew each other's secrets. I laughed as hard as the housewives.

"We've all seen Amrita's skinny little snake. It sleeps all day in her house, then roams around at night . . ."

"That's the snake I turned out of my house," said a recent bride, emboldened.

I didn't hear the rest of the taunt. I heard a growl, a kind of growling-and-stalking combination.

This dawn, as on many others, perverts from the village across the stream sat on their bank and ogled us. We knew they were there because the lit tips of their bidis floated like fireflies. We pretended they weren't there. They wanted to look, that's all; they never waded across, not even in the summer, when the sun dried up the stream like blotting paper.

The growl got louder, closer.

The men in our village weren't saints. We had our incidents. Rape, ruin, shame. The women's strategy was to stick together. Stragglers, beware. That morning I thought, Let it come. Let him pounce. I had the staff.

But that morning the enemy wasn't human. First I saw only the head. A pink-skinned, nearly hairless, twitching animal head. The head thrust itself through the bush, brambles stuck deep into its bleeding jowls.

Behind me women screamed. Water pots fell. Two women crawled, like crabs, loosened salwars around naked and frozen feet, toward the bank. Most were locked in a crouch. Fear stippled their naked haunches.

"Cowards!" I aimed my cry at the line of bidi smokers. "We know you are there! Please help us!"

The animal whipped its head back; the head was bloodied and monstrous. Then it started to drag itself noisily to the trash pit. A cow mulching garbage backed away. Peacocks hopped out of range. Only buzzards brooded from low-hanging trees; crows squawked.

"A mad dog!" I heard the women's chorus. "Help! Please help!"

A dog, but not a dog. It was bigger than a pariah, much bigger than a jackal, almost the size of a wolf. But this one didn't move like a wolf. It circled the pit, it sidled and snuck around like a jackal. A dog that dragged its hind legs. A dog that danced, jerkily, as it walked. The dog headed back for us. Its eyes glowed red, its slack jaws foamed.

I hated all dogs, distrusted their motives. I hated this dog because it had made terrified naked women crab-crawl.

The staff whacked brush.

The dog stopped twenty feet from me. It looked straight at me out of those red eyes. Then it spun on its front legs and squared off. Tremors raised pink ridges on its hairless sides. It stopped so close to me I could see flies stuck in the viscous drool. I knew it had come for me, not for the other women. It had picked me as its enemy. I wasn't ready to die. I'd seen a rabid man die horribly outside the mustached doctor's clinic.

I let the dog inch so close I could feel a slimy vapor spray out of its muzzle. I let it crouch and growl its low, terrible, gullety growl. I took aim and waited for it to leap on me.

The staff crushed the dog's snout while it was still in mid-leap. Spiny twigs hooked deep into its nostrils and split them open. I saw all this as I lay on the winter-hard ground.

The women helped me up. One of them poked the wounded animal with a twig. It lay on its back, its legs pumping outward like a turtle's. My staff was still stuck deep into the snout, its bloody tip poking through an eye socket. Blood plumed its raw sides. I'd never seen that much blood. The women dragged the body to the nullah and let it float away.

They brought me home and made a fuss over me. Dida said, "All it means is that God doesn't think you're ready for salvation. Individual effort counts for nothing." The next day, defeated, she left for her ashram.

9

PITAJI died the next May. He died horribly. He got off a
bus in a village two hours west of us and was gored by a
bull. He'd had the bus driver let him off in a country lane
so he could take a shortcut through a field to a friend's hut.
The friend he'd gone to visit was another Lahori, someone
he liked to play chess with. The horror was the suddenness.
He used to say, lying on his charpoy in the courtyard, I can
watch death coming from here. He'll have to be a very
sneaky fellow to catch me by surprise. I will die with my
kurta buttoned and my glasses folded on my paper and all
my prayers said. The bull attacked him from behind. He
never saw it coming.

The Lahori friend consoled my mother. "Why cry?

Crying is selfish. We have no husbands, no wives, no fathers, no sons. Family life and family emotions are all illusions. The Lord lends us a body, gives us an assignment, and sends us down. When we get the job done, the Lord calls us home again for the next assignment."

I know that sounds soft. "Very, very, *very* Indian, Jassy"—that's what Taylor used to say, back in Manhattan. "You don't believe that, do you? You can't, you're more modern than that."

What it means is this: Grant the notion that there's a God. Taylor agreed. For the sake of argument, then, if He's God, His assignments are perhaps too vast for the human mind, even your very superior one, Taylor. Go on, he said, smiling his lopsided, I'm-amused-by-all-this smile. Then, I said, let's make a bigger leap. Perhaps Pitaji's life assignment was merely to crunch one small piece of gravel as he jumped out of the bus that morning, and once he did it, perhaps God took the form of a maddened bull, or God took the form of nettles that caused a perfectly harmless bull enough pain to charge. Perhaps my father's assignment was to be just that: my father; to die in a freakish accident before he could marry me off so that I could be free to fall in love with Prakash. What if my father's assignment was to hasten my eloping with Prakash, hasten my getting to New York! Maybe *my* assignment was to bring you enlightenment, Taylor. Taylor laughed. Enlightenment? I remember him quizzing. So you think I'm a narrow-minded American bigot? I squeezed his square-knuckled fist to let him know I wasn't accusing him of bigotry. Enlightenment meant seeing through the third eye and sensing designs in history's muddles. I think now that maybe Pitaji's assignment was to strand me in Iowa, to bring me to Bud and to make possible the baby I am carrying, or to bring Du and me together in America. How do I explain my third eye to men who only see an inch-long pale, puckered scar?

Taylor sulked. He said, "Please, please don't ever call me a bigot." We talked about the work he was doing for Amnesty International. I cried when he described some South African torture methods. I kept crying because I'd been unfair to Taylor. I'd been horribly egotistical. Perhaps I don't count in God's design. Maybe Pitaji's assignment was merely to flee Lahore and provide a comfortable house for some Muslim gentleman and gold for someone's former servant. Maybe Pitaji's mission was to pluck a certain flower and release a certain seed. The scale of Brahma is vast, as vast as space in the universe. Why shouldn't our mission be infinitesimal? Aren't all lives, viewed that way, equally small? Only if we think of "assignment" as an important mission, something historical, was Pitaji a man unfulfilled.

I tried to explain this belief to Taylor, that a whole life's mission might be to move a flowerpot from one table to another; all the years of education and suffering and laughter, marriage, parenthood, education, serving merely to put a particular person in a particular room with a certain flower. If the universe is one room known only to God, then God alone knows how to furnish it, how to populate it.

Taylor was despondent that a grant application, to study the physical properties of a subatomic particle known to exist only in theory, had been rejected.

"I couldn't live in a world like yours," he said. "If rearranging a particle of dust is as important as discovering relativity, that's a formula for total anarchy. Total futility. Total fatalism. Where's the incentive to do anything?"

The incentive, I should have said, is to treat every second of your existence as a possible assignment from God. Everything you do, if you're a physicist or a caregiver, is equally important in the eye of God.

When Pitaji died, my mother tried to throw herself on his funeral pyre. When we wouldn't let her, she shaved her head with a razor, wrapped her body in coarse cloth, and sat all day in a corner. Once a day I force-fed spoonfuls of rice gruel into her.

10

Pitaji died in the hottest month, when the topsoil is so dry it grays and crumbles like ash. Arvind-prar and Hari-prar, who quit their technical school in Jullundhar to come back and look after us, sold the desiccated thirty-acre family ground and opened up a scooter-repair shop. They didn't talk anymore of going to Bahrain or Qatar. Like it or not, they were stuck in Hasnapur.

We didn't know it at the time but the man who bought our ground had already bought neighboring ground, so he ended up with a huge rhombus-shaped farm. He had gone to agricultural school in Canada, people said, and was testing out scientific ideas. Maybe it was science—he did plant a new kind of wheat—but I think mostly it was luck.

I used to take a roundabout route to the river so I could watch the new owner (we called him Vancouver Singh) at work. The late June sky, rough as steel wool, sent him greening rains at just the right time. The wrinkled soil muddied and squelched. Storks waded through wet fields. Thatch grass soared, saplings thickened. I watched Vancouver Singh, in his funny foreign yellow raincoat and boots, walk the raised paths my father had once walked. I felt robbed. I felt disconnected. I made a bonfire of my books under the jasmine tree. Even the bookworms and red ants didn't escape.

Sometime between winter and the next monsoon season, as the fields around us went from green to yellow to red and the air was fragrant with Vancouver Singh's harvest, my brothers started to bring home friends and clients. The guests were mostly tall, pleasant-looking Jat Hindu unmarried men. I knew what my brothers were up to, but I didn't let on. I served the sweet, frothy tea in heavy brass tumblers and snuck a look at them. I waited for sparks. I waited and waited.

What I liked was hearing the men talk. Their talk was always about vengeful, catastrophic politics. Sikh nationalists had gotten out of hand . . . The Khalsa Lions were making bombs . . . Kalashnikov- and Uzi-armed terrorists on mopeds were picking off the moderates, the police, innocent Hindus . . . Vancouver Singh's farm was a safehouse for drug pushers and gunmen . . . Punjab would explode in months, maybe even days . . . Hindus would be smart to get out while they could . . . The whole country was a bloody mess . . . In the sooty ocher light of clay lamps, impassioned men brought me the outside world of fatal hates. Evening by evening I felt less isolated. I started listening to the All-India Radio English-language newscast again, the first time since Pitaji died, and borrowing Vimla's father's copy of *The Hindu*. How much English, how quickly, I'd forgotten!

Even in Hasnapur things started to happen. A transistor radio blew up in the bazaar. A busload of Hindus on their way to a shrine to Lord Ganpati was hijacked and all males shot dead at point-blank range.

One day my brothers brought home a man from our village whom they'd known in school, and then in Jullundhar, a baptized Sikh who wore his beard the way the Khalsa Lions did, long and full and stiffly combed out over his chest. Masterji had always worn his rolled and netted. The man had unforgiving eyes, maybe that's what made me wary of him right away. I brought him a glass of water and a glass of sweet tea, but he didn't touch either, as if drinking anything in our impure, infidel home would contaminate him.

Hari-prar and Arvind-prar didn't seem to feel the same way, and they got started on their boisterous political arguments about the future of our state more quickly than usual. I felt, though, that the talk that night had more ferocious threats, interruptions, curses than jokes and laments, so I went indoors and tried to comfort, or at least reach, Mataji, by massaging her razored-rough head.

But even indoors I couldn't shut out the flat, authoritative voice of the new guest. The Khalsa, the Pure-Bodied and the Pure-Hearted, must have their sovereign state. Khalistan, the Land of the Pure. The Impure must be eliminated. My brothers laughed. "How, Sukkhi? You're not going to kill brothers from your own village."

"You must leave, then. Leave or be killed. Renounce all filth and idolatry. Do not eat meat, smoke tobacco, or drink alcohol or cut your hair. Wear a turban, and then you will be welcome."

"What kind of choice is that? That's worse than the Muslims gave."

"Is there anything else you want us to do, Sukkhi?" asked Arvind-prar.

"Yes. Keep your whorish women off the streets."

I expected a fight—people had died over less—but my brothers must have been in a good mood. Maybe they just didn't believe what they were hearing. "Sukhwinder, where do they teach you such nonsense?"

"I have visited Sant Bhindranwale in the Golden Temple."

"The Sant's an idiot." Bhindranwale was the leader of all the fanatics.

Later that night I heard a scooter roar into our courtyard. The arguments became more personal. The new voice spoke without rushing and exclaiming, and when it said, "You're a fool, Sukkhi," which it did quite often, a laugh prologued the indictment.

Sukhwinder didn't tire, he just grew louder. He called all Hindu women whores, all Hindu men rapists. "The sari is the sign of the prostitute," he said. And "Hindus are bent on genocide of the Sikh nation. Only Pakistan protects us."

The new man, whom my brothers called Prakash, kept pushing. He said, in that sharp laughing way of his, "Sukkhi, there's no Hindu state! There's no Sikh state! India is for everyone. Have you forgotten what the Muslims did to Sikhs in Partition? What the Moghuls did to your own Ten Gurus? Have you forgotten what Emperor Aurangzeb did, what Emperor Jehangir did?"

I fell in love with that voice. It was low, gravelly, unfooled. I was prepared to marry the man who belonged to that voice.

"They were Moghuls, not Muslims!" Sukhwinder could only register helplessness and peevishness.

"Not Muslims, Sukkhi? I don't think they worshipped Jesus Christ," said the new man.

"They were Afghan slaves, not true Pakistanis. True Pakistanis are Punjabis, like us. If they were cruel to Sikhs, it's because of Hindu influence on them. Many of them had Hindu mothers and Hindu concubines who taught them to kill Sikhs. Pakistanis were Hindus who saw the light of the true God and converted. So were Sikhs. Only bloodsucker banyas and untouchable monkeys remained Hindu."

The man I meant to marry snapped back, "What absolute rubbish you speak. You've lost your mind. Don't talk nonsense about the light of the true God. They had to convert or have their heads chopped off." Then he must have turned to my brothers, because he said, "This man is a danger to us and to himself."

Sukhwinder did some saber-banging and cursing, then whooshed off on his scooter. The other man stayed on. There were cracks in my door, but the light was too low to see anything. Only a very tall, very strong man could have a voice like that.

That rowdy insomniac evening I didn't leave the hut, and I didn't see Prakash, but I learned more facts about him. He was a city boy from Amritsar, the city of the Sikhs' Golden Temple, which meant he'd seen more Hindu-Sikh clashes than we had in our little village. He was a good student, about to graduate, about to send away job applications to Germany and the United States. "You can keep the Emirates," he said dismissively. "When I go to work in another country, it'll be because I want to be a part of it. Can you imagine working in a place like Qatar? That's blood money they pay you. You come back a rich slave. I wouldn't go just to be a guest worker, and I wouldn't go because I was afraid of the Sukkhis putting bullets in our heads."

Then they went on to shoptalk. Prakash seemed to have a special talent for fixing televisions, VCRs, computers. My brothers, muscled and uncomplicated mechanics, liked to lug big greasy machine parts, and afterward quaff down quart bottles of Kingfisher beer, while Prakash sounded more like a surgeon, a confident professional in starched white, lifting microchips with wire forceps.

Love rushes through thick mud walls. Love before first sight: that's our Hasnapuri way.

11

THE next morning I packed my brothers' tiffin carriers more indulgently than usual—extra dal, extra chapatis, extra pickles and chillies and lemon wedges—and slipped in my most important question: "The friend who came over, not the Sardarji, does he speak English?" I couldn't marry a man who didn't speak English, or at least who didn't want to speak English. To want English was to want more than you had been given at birth, it was to want the world.

"First-class English," Hari-prar said. "You think he has a little sister to translate manuals for him?"

Arvind-prar added, "Prakash isn't a dunderhead like us. He'll move to America in a year or two. He already has friends in New York. He knows ways."

After that for almost two weeks they said no more about Prakash. I didn't even know his last name.

I went about the day trying not to show how I felt. I wouldn't redden, I wouldn't hum film songs under my breath. I boiled the milk, cleaned the chicken coop, supervised the Mazbi maidservant, shopped, cooked, bathed, and fed Mataji, did the chores I had to do. And in the siesta hour I sat with old copies of newspapers and practiced English phrases. "The time has come for this great nation to be a greater nation by eschewing indiscriminate use of foreign expertise and technology." I liked the word "eschewing." I copied it several times over in the exercise book I hadn't taken out of the shallow-shelved, built-in cabinet since I'd abandoned Masterji. Red ants had gotten into the book's binding. I felt ready to leave for Germany, the States. It didn't occur to me that Germans didn't speak English.

And then, after about three weeks, just as I was beginning to worry that Prakash was a phantom, a voice without a body, Hari-prar stumped into the hut whistling "I Love You," my favorite song from *Mr. India*, and slipped three movie tickets into my fist. "I got first-class seats," he boasted, shaking rain off his hair. "Nine p.m. showing tomorrow. But get ready early. You know how crazy the rickshaw wallas and the bidi wallas are for Sanjay Dutt."

I toweled dry his wide spiky head. He had said nothing about Prakash, but I knew that if they had spent money on a movie ticket for me, they meant for their friend to bump into me. I was a sister without dowry, but I didn't have to be a sister without prospects.

That night the rain thickened into a downpour. I sat on Mataji's sleeping mat and hugged her. We listened together to the rain soften the dirt in our courtyard. Mataji tented her quilt around me; it was her bridal quilt, the red cotton cover tattered, the stuffing thin and lumpy. I smelled mildew. Moonlight and monsoon dampness fought their way in through the small window. Ours was the only kaccha house on the lane to have a window. It wasn't a real window, not like the big rectangles with glass and wrought-iron grilles in Vimla's house; it was just a crude gap in the mud wall. But to my Lahori father it had been a "window," because to live windowless was to live like an insect, he said, to give up. I couldn't see the neem tree from where I sat, but I could smell its bitter clean leaves and the heady ammonia of fresh mud. Good things were about to happen. I would carry out Mataji's forgotten mission.

The next dawn I let the maidservant's little girl scavenge firewood and light the hearth and boil the milk. I didn't want scratched arms, red eyes, and smoky hair. Effect must be calculated. I braided my hair three different ways. From my mother's rusted-out trunk, I extracted one of her few Lahore saris, a pale peach silk embroidered all over with gold leaves. I added Pitaji's dark glasses—I would put them on only when we got to the cinema house. At the last minute, I stuck a jasmine wreath in my hair.

I have no idea how I looked that night—the only mirror in our hut was a rearview rectangle that Arvind-prar had twisted off a UN jeep he'd found rusting in the demilitarized zone near the border—but I know how I felt. A goddess couldn't have been surer. At the bottom of the mirror were some English words I didn't exactly understand but took as a kind of mantra:

OBJECTS IN MIRROR ARE CLOSER
THAN THEY APPEAR

We rode Hari-prar's scooter over sticky and rutted kaccha roads, Hari-prar steering and Arvind-prar holding a tarp over our heads to keep us from some of the rain. The roads closer to the bazaar were paved and slick. The scooter skidded only once, spilling Arvind-prar into a construction pit where an American-style "super bazaar" was being put up by Potatoes-babu with some money from Vancouver Singh. Arvind-prar's khaki pants got khakier with mud. "Son of a pig!" he yelled at the pit. "Baboon!"

When we got to the movie theater, people were already massed outside the door, but Hari-prar decided we'd arrived too early and led us into a tea shop across the street. The tea shop had been a garage not long before, and still looked it. The owner had dropped out of the same technical college in Jullundhar as had my brothers, and at about the same time, so there was some backslapping to get through before we were seated at the best table, just out of the rain but with the fullest view of the sidewalk.

The owner was a conspicuously charming man, but his

wasn't the voice that had seduced me weeks ago. I put on the dark glasses to look movie-starrish and scanned the tables for the man I was supposed to accidentally bump into. I didn't come up with a single possibility.

"You are so kind to grace my humble shop." The owner was at our table, ordering the small boys and old men who did the serving to bring cleaner glasses, hotter tea, spoons for the gulab jamuns. He paid me more compliments. "What, you are trying only one spoonful of my world-famous sweets? A pretty lady always has a delicate appetite?"

Our waiter, a stooped old man in khaki shorts that didn't hide warty growths on one thigh, served me steaming tea in a cup with a saucer. Everyone else got tea in glasses. I read the sign: I was special. I was a pretty lady with delicate taste, not a dowryless fourteen-year-old. I poured a little tea into the saucer as I had seen Vimla do many times, and blew and sipped and blew some more.

The tea was barely warm enough to fog up the bottom rim of my sunglasses, and it was weak. I brewed better tea.

A bald man two tables away joked, "Kapoor sahib is trying hard to impress someone."

I was meant to hear the joke. Did that mean that the man with the laugh in his voice had shown no interest at all? That this evening wasn't planned for Prakash, whose last name I still didn't know?

The owner bumped my shoulder, faking clumsiness, on his way back to the kitchen to scold the cook. "Pardon me, pardon me. I am an oaf!"

I stopped sipping. The tea had cooled enough for a patch of brownish skin to form in the middle of the cup. I did not want to spend my life with an oaf who had to fake an accident in order to touch me.

The moviegoers were now massed on the street and on both sidewalks. They fluted around vendors' stalls and pressed into our tea shop. One man about Arvind-prar's age walked past (a little too casually, I thought) and looked at me (again, a little too casually). I stared back. He walked back the way he had come, or tried to. The movie line's swelling and rippling forced a stumble out of him. When I gasped (I hadn't meant to), he swiveled back to smile at me. A thin lock of hair tumbled out of place, over one eye. He was not a tall man, and his mustache was neatly trimmed in a thin bar, like my brothers'. An impression was all I had: dignity, kindness, intelligence. Maybe even humor.

Why did I get the needy, ingratiating charmers and oafs instead?

Hari-prar checked his Seiko—a present from a customer whose smuggled Toyota he'd fixed—and asked for the check.

"You want to insult me? You think I'd charge you money when you have brought me however brief a presence of this lovely lady?"

We gathered our umbrellas and flashlights. The rest of the night seemed unstoppable and unbearable. Three hours or more in soggy clothes in an over-air-conditioned hall, men copping feels in the chilly dark, mice scurrying under seats for warmth.

"Arvind!"

I clutched my flashlight.

"So, you *do* think she's a temptress? You took so long we thought she'd failed the test!"

The stumbler floated toward me.

"What is your name?" He asked the question in English. He asked it in a very soft voice.

"Arré," Arvind-prar objected. "You know her name already."

But the voice kept welling over me. "Does she talk? What is your name?"

"Answer him!" Arvind-prar ordered. "She is all the time talking, we can hardly shut her up."

"Shut up," he said, not unkindly, in Punjabi. "She is blushing. She is a woman of fine sympathies, not like you blockheads. You *are* blushing. Are you afraid of me? There is time to talk. I saw you worry, back there, when I stumbled. It was instinctive, wasn't it? Don't talk. Don't say a word. I want to be surprised when I hear your voice."

12

Two weeks later we were married. I wore Mataji's red and gold wedding sari, which was only slightly damaged by mold, and in my hair the sweetest-smelling jasmines. Ours was a no-dowry, no-guests Registry Office wedding in a town a 250-rupee taxi ride south of Hasnapur. Vimla, who was engaged to the son of the Tractor King of our district (he imported Zetta tractors from Czechoslovakia and was supposed to have illegal bank accounts all over Europe), accused us of living in sin. I showed her our marriage certificate, but she shook her head. She said, "It isn't for me to say anything like this, I know, and of course the papers nowadays are full of caste-no-bar–divorcees-welcome matrimonial ads, but it seems to me that once you let one tradition go, all the other traditions crumble."

She and her fiancé were holding off their marriage till he was twenty, because of their horoscopes. "What is the sacrifice of a little bliss now for a guaranteed lifetime?" Just because you're clever in school doesn't mean you can ignore your fate in the stars, she reminded me. I'd already had my warning, which I succeeded in blocking ("Believe an old fool?" "What does he know? Ha!") every time the memory of the banyan tree and the old man came over me in the night.

My husband, Prakash Vijh, was a modern man, a city man. He did trash some traditions, right from the beginning. For instance, in Jullundhar, instead of moving in with his uncle's family, as the uncle had expected us to— Prakash had lost his parents in a cholera epidemic when he was ten—he rented a two-room apartment in a three-story building across the street from the technical college. His uncle fussed: "In the old days we had big houses and big families. Now nobody cares for old people," and his aunt wept: "Your wife is so fancy that our place isn't good enough for her?" The Prime Minister was destroying ancient values with her vasectomy program and giving out free uterine loops.

But Prakash remained impatient. "There's no room in modern India for feudalism," he declared.

For the uncle, love was control. Respect was obedience. For Prakash, love was letting go. Independence, self-reliance: I learned the litany by heart. But I felt suspended between worlds.

*   *   *

He wanted me to call him by his first name. "Only in feudal societies is the woman still a vassal," he explained. "Hasnapur is feudal." In Hasnapur wives used only pronouns to address their husbands. The first months, eager and obedient as I was, I still had a hard time calling him Prakash. I'd cough to get his attention, or start with "Are you listening?" Every time I coughed he'd say, "Do I hear a crow trying human speech?" Prakash. I had to practice and practice (in the bathroom, in the tarped-over corner of the verandah which was our kitchen) so I could say the name without gagging and blushing in front of his friends. He liked to show me off. His friends were like him: disrupters and rebuilders, idealists.

Pygmalion wasn't a play I'd seen or read then, but I realize now how much of Professor Higgins there was in my husband. He wanted to break down the Jyoti I'd been in Hasnapur and make me a new kind of city woman. To break off the past, he gave me a new name: Jasmine. He said, "You are small and sweet and heady, my Jasmine. You'll quicken the whole world with your perfume."

Jyoti, Jasmine: I shuttled between identities.

We had our arguments. "We aren't going to *spawn*! We aren't ignorant peasants!" Prakash yelled every time I told him that I wanted to get pregnant. I was past fifteen, and girls in the village, and my mother, were beginning to talk. He said he was too poor to start a family and I was too young. My kind of feudal compliance was what still kept India an unhealthy and backward nation. It was up to the women to resist, because men were generally too greedy and too stupid to recognize their own best interests. I didn't dare confess that I felt eclipsed by the Mazbi maid's daughter, who had been married off at eleven, just after me, and already had had a miscarriage.

"Just because you're a good engineering student you think you know everything," I fought back. "You think that hi-tech solves every problem. What does hi-tech say about a woman's need to be a mother?"

He said, "It says you are still very young and foolish. It says you are confusing social and religious duty with instinct. I honor the instinct, and there is nothing more inevitable than a fourteen-year-old married woman becoming a mother." But he didn't put real venom into it. And he didn't hit me—he never hit me.

Instead, he'd ask, "What's ten divided by two?"

"Five. You think I've forgotten how to count?"

"And what's ten divided by ten?"

"One. I'm not dumb."

"And which number is larger, five or one?"

There was no winning these arguments. He'd read more than I had. He had statistics for everything. He'd done more thinking than I had; he was twenty-four and I was fifteen, a village fifteen, ready to be led. He was an engineer, not just of electricity, he said, but of all the machinery in the world, seen and unseen. It all ran by rules, if we just understood them. The important thing, he said, was to keep arguing, fight him if I didn't agree. We shouldn't do anything if we didn't both agree.

So we didn't start a family. My poor, good-hearted

husband! I think now that he was afraid of hurting me, afraid of embarrassing me with any desire or demand. "Jasmine, Jasmine," he would whisper in the anguished intimacy of our little room, "help me be a better person."

And I did. I bit him and nibbled him and pressed his head against my bosom.

Prakash left the apartment before five-thirty in the morning six days a week and didn't get home before eight or nine in the evening. He worked two jobs, one as a repairman and bookkeeper for Jagtiani and Son Electrical Goods, and the other as a math tutor to a dreamy boy of thirteen. Then he crammed for his diploma exams. I missed him, but I didn't feel abandoned. Abandonment meant deliberate withdrawal; his was absence. He had to pay rent, buy expensive technical books, save so we could start our family. He was a shameless saver.

I found things to do all day without trying. For instance, there was a Ladies' Group raffle in our building and I was asked to take over its running. And then Parminder in flat 2B said that since I had no in-laws and no infants to harass me all day, why didn't I go with her on her door-to-door detergent-selling routes in three neighborhood buildings and she would cut me in. The commission I kept secret from Prakash. He was a modern man. Still, I wasn't sure how he would react to my having my own kitty.

*   *   *

Sundays were our days together. Mr. Jagtiani couldn't buy Prakash on Sundays, not even with promises of off-the-record double overtime. Mr. Jagtiani, like Potatoes-babu and other traders, did some of his business in black money that didn't appear in the books and some in taxable white. Prakash hated having to keep the books for Mr. Jagtiani. "I'm an inventor," he grumbled, "I shouldn't have to lie and cheat and be that louse's accomplice!" Prakash grumbled, I consoled. We were content.

In good weather we could ride deep into the countryside on his scooter. Beggars with broken bodies shoved alms bowls at suited men in automobiles. Shacks sprouted like toadstools around high-rise office buildings. Camels loped past satellite dishes. Centuries coalesced as we picnicked.

"I feel lucky," I often whispered as I rode pillion. Prakash had a secondhand Bajaj scooter which he'd fixed up himself. I *was* lucky. Vimla's avaricious husband-to-be with the perfect horoscope was demanding a red Maruti car from Potatoes-babu.

"Foolish woman." Prakash laughed. "Someday I'll be able to make you genuinely happy."

One late Sunday night—he'd been cramming for the exams in bed and I'd started out the night helping by massaging his neck and shoulders and then, I guess, fallen asleep—he shook me awake roughly.

"You're ill?" I gasped, scrambling to a sitting position

inside our mosquito net. Prakash looked awful. I hadn't seen him that confused or gloomy. "You *are* ill!"

"Yes," he said. He dropped his head heavily on the pillow. "Yes, I'm ill." He tapped his heart. "Ill here."

He untucked the mosquito net and pushed himself off the bed. I heard the buzz of greedy bugs. He went out to the porch for boiled water. He gulped two aspirin, and brought two more back for me.

"Jasmine, what do you think of America?"

I didn't know what to think of America. I'd read only *Shane*, and seen only one movie. It was too big a country, too complicated a question. I said, "If you're there, I'll manage. When you're at work in America, I'll stay inside."

He let out one of his long, exasperated sighs.

"What should I have said?"

"Listen to me, Jasmine. I want for us to go away and have a real life. I've had it up to here with backward, corrupt, mediocre fools."

Mr. Jagtiani must have asked him to cook the books again. "All right," I said, "if you want me to have a real life, I want it, too."

"Arré, maybe I shouldn't have asked. *You* have to want to go away, too. *You* have to want to have a real life."

"What is this real life? I have a real life."

But his head slackened onto my pillow. For the rest of the night, I faked sleep.

* * *

81

A week later Prakash came home drunk. I'd seen my brothers drunk, but never Prakash. My brothers were rowdy drunks, Prakash was melancholy. He laid his textbooks out in a row on the bed. I hated what the job at Mr. Jagtiani's was doing to him.

"Let me get you Andrew's Liver Salt," I said.

"You think everything can be fixed with Andrew's Liver Salt."

"Don't work for that man anymore," I begged. "You're an engineer, not a lackey." Impulsively I showed him the empty tin of biscuits in which I hoarded my savings from the detergent route. Parminder could be talked into giving me my own route, a longer one.

"You secretive little monkey!" he shouted.

I panicked. For all his talk of us being equal, was he possessive about my working? I remembered how on Sundays when the Bajaj chugged us along pedestrian-packed streets, he imagined strange lewd hands grabbing at me and pinching. We'd been married under a year. My mother always warned me that a husband has layers, like an onion, and you'll still find things to surprise you, usually bad things—since men show off their good side very early—years and years after you marry. Maybe he was possessive and jealous and even a secret drunk, reeling around the bedroom trying not to spill a glass of antacid, and I was stuck with him.

"Oh, that bloodsucker again?" I asked.

"No, that bloodsucking Sindhi has nothing to do with what I'm feeling." Then, like a magician groping in a top hat for a new trick—Masterji had once taken our whole class to the Gandhi Auditorium in the bazaar to see Marvelous Mahendra, the Maharaja of Magic, and we had loved Marvelous Mahendra more than we had the American movie *Seven Village Girls Find Seven Boys to Marry*—he whipped an aerogram out of his trouser pocket and flicked me with it.

How velvety the paper felt on my forearm and wrist! Our aerograms were rough and fibrous, you had to gouge your sentences into the paper. CELEBRATE AMERICA, the American postal services commanded. TRAVEL . . . THE PERFECT FREEDOM. "Read," he said. "I should be sending, not receiving, letters from Kissena Boulevard, Flushing, Queens."

The letter was from a Professor Devinder Vadhera. I knew that Professor Vadhera had taught Prakash his first year in the technical college, and that he'd lent Prakash money for books, college fees, examination fees, tiffin, bus fare, everything, out of his own less-than-nothing instructor-level salary, so Prakash could stay in school.

"Without this man, I'd be like your brothers. I'd be just tinkering and tampering."

Devinder Vadhera's letter was in English. I handed it back to my husband. "You read it to me," I said.

"What's the matter? You've forgotten all the English Masterji dinned into you? You've become like the others, my little flower?" There was a slurred, nasty edge to his voice, nothing playful, and his eyes were red. "Caring only about pregnancies?"

It was unfair. I had no books, no magazines, I reminded him.

"Then study the technical textbooks and manuals I bring home every night!"

He read me only the part he wanted me to hear.

Day by day our Jullundhar graduates are rushing to this country and minting lakhs and lakhs of rupees. They stay in nice houses with 24-hour electricity and no load shedding. They have running hot and cold water. They and their wives also are liking to work. They enjoy all manner of comforts and amenities. I see the onrush of the dunderheads from our college. When will I see my truly best student blooming in the healthy soil of this country?

Professor Vadhera, still the benefactor, went on to list two technical institutes (both with "International" in the name and both in Florida) which, for a fee, made it easy for international students to get their visas and which also negotiated a very generous exchange of Jullundhar college credits.

"You heard that," Prakash said, after he'd finished reading. "I was his best student. The rest were dunderheads. Dunderheads! You see how the mediocre are smart enough to get away? Only we, the best ones, let ourselves be hemmed in by bloodsuckers and dunderheads."

"We'll go to America," I said, helping him out of his clothes and into bed. I laid a dampened washcloth over his eyes and forehead and sprinkled cologne on it. He smelled of beer. Like my brothers. My brothers were good men, but they weren't imaginative and they weren't ambitious. All they had were nearly harmless consolatory vices. They would never get away to the emirates, and they knew it. They drank and gambled to forget they once upon a time had wanted to. My husband was obsessed with passing exams, doing better, making something more of his life than fate intended.

I heard melancholy snores. I thought of the old man under the banyan tree. If we could just get away from India, then all fates would be canceled. We'd start with new fates, new stars. We could say or be anything we wanted. We'd be on the other side of the earth, out of God's sight.

One day back in Hasnapur, my mother told me, when the children were gathered under the banyan in the school-yard, a scooter started sputtering and backfiring very close to Masterji's desk on the raised dais he called his stage. He tolerated the interference as long as he could, then stopped the class and walked over to the boys, who were just sitting on the scooter, firing up the engine and letting it throb. He got about ten feet from them, and then spun around and started running back toward the class. The boys gave chase and caught him without much effort. In front of the students they first knocked his turban off. They called him insulting names. He started crying and holding his beard and his exposed white hair in his hands. "I am a good Sikh, a pious Sikh," he cried. "Why are you doing this?

We are peaceful people." They pulled out the ceremonial comb, and his life-long hair fell over his shoulders, down his back. The boys were laughing, and the students didn't know what to do. While one boy barbered the teacher, chopping at the hair in great clumps, another held a machine gun over the children.

After they freed his rolled-up beard and chopped it off, they spun him around until he staggered and fell. Then they shot him, emptying over thirty bullets in him, according to the police inspector.

13

THE next afternoon, instead of helping the Ladies'
Group with their weekly raffle, I lay across the bed and
flipped through the thinnest of Prakash's manuals. He had
books, papers, manuals, charts, stacked in neat rows on the
bed as well as under it; we slept across the width of the
mattress so we wouldn't knock down the Prakash Vijh Technical Library. The diploma exams—preparing for them,
passing them with first-class honors—obsessed him.

The manual was for a VCR that Mr. Jagtiani had smuggled back from Dubai and that he had wrecked trying to
hook up by himself. Prakash was having to work on it at
home so that Mrs. Jagtiani, whom we'd never met, could
record a popular religious show that weekend. Prakash

hated bringing a conspicuous electronic item like a VCR home because burglars were likely to be tempted. There were no secrets in our building. People kept their windows open and their televisions and stereos blaring. What was the point of owning high-status goods if nobody knew you owned them? Punjabis were so rich! We hadn't seen it all happening in the village, but in the towns, every little flat had a television set, and everyone had a close relative in Canada or the United States bringing back the latest gadgets.

That's what excited Prakash about electronics. It was a frontier, especially in India, and no one was staying back to service the goods that were flooding in. A good repairman would eventually make a fortune, even in Jullundhar. And an inventive one could devise electronics using native skill and native resources and designed for native conditions. He was basically an old-fashioned Indian patriot, with a lot of Gandhi and a lot of Nehru in him.

Lately, the burglaries had gotten out of hand. Clock radios, Cuisinarts, sewing machines disappeared every day. Some people said the Khalsa Lions—the Lions in Jullundhar were older and bolder than the ones in the village—were behind the break-ins. The rumor was that the Lions didn't just pass the goods on to a fence. They were converting them into homemade bombs to blow up shops and buses. Having the VCR in the house, Prakash complained, was begging for burglars.

*   *   *

I read his grumbling as self-hate. He hated himself for wasting his precious cramming time on freebies for Blood-sucker Jagtiani. At least the manual would help me scour the rust off my English. I started reading. By the time I finished, it was dark, it was time to bathe and change into a fresh kameez and light the butane and fry up pakoras.

Prakash said, "So your mind hasn't deteriorated after all. I've got you hooked, have I?"

That evening was a turning point in our marriage. He had read aloud from the manual as he worked. "Here," he said, "your hands are smaller. Lift this." He gave me a pair of delicate pliers and guided them through a maze of tiny lines and wires. In bed he said, "I like having you near me when I work. We'll have to open our own store someday."

"Bigger than Jagtiani and Son." I laughed.

"Vijh & Wife," my husband said from deep inside my embrace. "Maybe even Vijh & Vijh."

These were happy times for us. Prakash brought home ruined toasters, alarm clocks, calculators, electric fans, and I learned to probe and heal. We lived for our fantasy. Vijh & Wife!

Vijh & Vijh. Vijh & Sons.

But these were unhappy times for the city. Radios burst into flames on store shelves. Cars blew up on the street. The scared swapped tips: the Lions don't always wear beards and turbans—just the steel bracelet. They can look like you and me. We started looking first at the wrist, before getting closer.

Then came confusing times. One day in April, Prakash said, very casually, "Well, it came through. You're looking at a bona-fide student-to-be of the Florida International Institute of Technology." He pulled a manila folder out of his briefcase but didn't hand it to me. "Tam-pah," he said. It sounded like a Punjabi village name, the way he pronounced it. Even now I think of it that way. Tampah.

He showed me the brochure. *Admission obtained, future guaranteed.* Two young Indian or Pakistani men and two Chinese or Japanese women on the cover were standing under palm trees, smiling in their white shirts. Everyone on the cover and in the pictures inside was Indian or Chinese, with a couple of Africans. It didn't look anything like the America I'd read about. "You don't have to worry about me—it says 'Indian food readily available.' The Admissions Director is from the south. Ramaswamy."

"Why didn't you tell me you'd applied?"

"I didn't tell you in case I failed. I don't share losses, only winnings."

"What rubbish is that?"

"Always in such a hurry, Jasmine. You have a whole lifetime to share my losses. The husband must protect the wife whenever he can. Where is it written that a sixteen-year-old girl can share a man's losses? Such a man should be put in jail."

"But I will be seventeen soon. When do we leave?"

"You might be eighteen before this visa comes through. You think going to America is as easy as going to Bombay or Delhi?"

Then he told me about American visas, how he'd have to prove to suspicious Embassy officials that I was legally married to him and that he had enough dollars to support me, and of course the foreign exchange was tricky because the arrangements with Devinder Vadhera would have to be hush-hush, illegal, sleazy, unfortunately necessary, just like the black-money bookkeeping for Mr. Jagtiani. He'd also have to lie about my age. I'd have to be eighteen, at least, maybe nineteen, since they'd assume we were lying. Give them a year or two so they could take it away.

"I can't live without you," I said. I realized the moment I said it how true it had become. My life before Prakash, the girl I had been, the village, were like a dream from another life.

He laughed. "Save it for the movies. I'll send for you quickly, you'll see. You'll go back to your mother and write me every week from Hasnapur. Hari will scooter your letter directly to the post office. I'll be one of those boys in a white shirt with a blue aerogram in his pocket."

"Standing next to a Chinese girl."

"Look how ugly they are. Really, Jasmine, I am a faithful husband and dedicated student."

"There will be all those hot-blooded American girls. You know what they're like."

We flipped through the pages of the brochure. "Not here," he said. We had a big laugh. "I don't think they let Americans in!" We giggled at all the pictures, all the white shirts and mustaches. We made up names for all the stiff-backed, pompous-looking Indians. "*Must* be a Bengali," he'd say, "No? I am a very good Bengali boy. My name is Babu Banerjee and I eat rabri and hilsa fish three times a day." And "Oh, look at that crafty, ratlike pair of eyes. Sindhi, I'll bet. Mr. Moneyani." For the first time in my life I was looking at familiar Indian faces and seeing them as strange, a kind of tribe of intense men with oily hair, heavy-rimmed glasses, and mustaches.

I knew he was a faithful husband, that he loved me, but I could be jealous of even the air around him if I wasn't there. "If you leave me, I'll jump into a well."

He laughed again and told me to stop regressing into the feudal Jyoti. "You are Jasmine now. You can't jump into wells!" Then he ducked under the bed and pulled out a suitcase that I hadn't seen because of the books piled in front of it. The suitcase smelled of some new man-made material. Inside it was just one thing: a neatly folded light blue Teriwool suit with a label, BABUR ALI/MASTER TAILOR/JULLUNDHAR, on the sleeve.

And so, that hot cloudless April evening we rode the Bajaj through streets that seemed oddly empty, to the fanciest sari shop in the bazaar, where all the customers were paunchy perfectionists and all the shop assistants shameless flatterers.

"Show us your wedding saris," Prakash commanded.

He seated himself by the doorway to catch the slightest, driest breeze.

I felt rich, prized, a queen. A sari for the co-owner of Vijh & Wife. I draped gold-threaded silks over each shoulder and moved toward the wall mirror. It was the beginning of the real life we wanted, needed, to live.

I was looking in the mirror and saying, "Prakash, I've made my pick, but I want you to guess which one; I want to know how good we are at telepathy, so we can talk to each other across the seas . . ." and Prakash was taking out the bills he kept neatly folded in his shirt pocket, when a shadow blackened the naphtha lamp on the stool by the shop's door.

Two Lions, one of them carrying a music box, lounged in the doorway. And then, behind them, something moved, a slight man on a motor scooter. I saw the man's face, Sukhwinder's face, Sukkhi's, only something was different. It was wrong somehow. Sukkhi wasn't wearing a turban. His hair was burry short, his face baby smooth.

I swung around. "Prakash, look!" The Lions had left their music box just inside the door. On the sidewalk Sukhwinder's motor scooter sputtered and growled.

Instant replay in slow motion. I can't turn the VCR off. The sidewalk surges, men scream. I am screaming. My hands touch a red wet cheek, my eyes are closed, Prakash and I stumble together, Sukkhi guns the motor, shouting, "Prostitutes! Whores!"

I failed you. I didn't get there soon enough. The bomb was meant for me, prostitute, whore.

I let myself fall to the floor. Voices girdle me. "The girl's alive. This is fate. This is a miracle!" My husband's body cushions me. They can't pry us apart, we're that close.

In the police car, the officer said, "I'm very sorry. You'll have to do the identifying."

I clutched his sleeve. "I saw the man. I saw it happen." Rosettes of blood bloomed on the sleeve of the officer's stiff-starched uniform. I touched him again to make more rosettes bloom.

"Identification of your respected late spouse," he explained. He held open a plastic sack with the sari shop's name printed on it. "This is your late husband's watch, isn't it? Just a nod will do for identification."

I put my hand inside the sack, but the man stopped me. "Now is evidence for forensic investigation only. Also, sometimes, legal questions are raised with respect to deceased's jewelries and other valuables. In the case of a deceased married woman, for instance, is her dowry jewelry properly returned to her parents, the dowry givers, or is it the property of her husband or, in the case of multiple death, of the husband's parents? You see how my hands are tied."

I heard a woman's terrible scream. "If you can't give me what's mine, at least shut up and do your job right. I saw the man." I clawed the officer and the officer tapped the horn. "Sukkhi. Sukhwinder. From the Vocational College in town. I saw his face in the mirror."

"Yes, yes, madam." He meant to soothe me. "We will pursue every lead in this heinous act. One by one we are hunting down the miscreants."

"Kill him!" There was that terrible scream again. "At least do your job right and kill him!"

14

THINK Vijh & Wife! Prakash exhorted me from every corner of our grief-darkened room. There is no dying, there is only an ascending or a descending, a moving on to other planes. Don't crawl back to Hasnapur and feudalism. That Jyoti is dead.

My sisters all were living in cities, with jealous, drunken men who wouldn't part with a few rupees of bus or train fare. They were gone from my life. Except for the visits of my brothers on the weekends, Mataji and I were alone in the widow's dark hut, little better than Mazbis and Untouchables. My young friends, like Vimla, never visited. Inexplicable, seemingly undeserved misfortune is contagious. She didn't want her unblemished young life in any way marred. *A bull and a bomb have made them widows, mother and daughter! How they must have sinned to suffer so now!* My mother kept company only with other widows, bent old women of public humility and secret bitterness. I felt myself dead in their company, with my long hair and schoolgirl clothes. I wanted to scream, "Feudalism! I am a widow in the war of feudalisms."

I grieved. I read slokas with swamis in mountainside ashrams. For every fish, there is a fisherman; for every deer a hunter. For every monster a hero. Our highest mission, said a swami, is to create new life. How many children do you have? When I bowed my head, he offered prayer.

Later, I thought, We *had* created life. Prakash had taken Jyoti and created Jasmine, and Jasmine would complete the mission of Prakash. Vijh & Wife. A vision had formed. There were thousands of useless rupees in our account. He had his Florida acceptance and his American visa. I turned everything over to my brothers, along with my plan. They were stupefied. A village girl, going alone to America, without job, husband, or papers? I must be mad! Certainly, I was. I told them I had sworn it before God. A matter of duty and honor. I dared not tell my mother.

Dida came down from her ashram. For once, the women agreed. My mother and I should stay together, two widows shopping and cooking for each other, keeping the shrines of their husbands alive. Dida didn't need to read slokas for my edification: she had her own vast store of knowledge.

If you had married the widower in Ludhiana that was all arranged . . . If you had checked the boy's horoscope and not married like a Christian in some government office . . . If you had waited for a man I picked . . . none of this would have happened. I am told you called him by his proper name. It is very clear. You were in the sari shop to buy something you could not afford, to celebrate a separation from your husband and his desertion of India to make money abroad. God was displeased. God sent that Sardarji boy to do that terrible thing.

Dida, I said, if God sent Sukkhi to kill my husband, then I renounce God. I spit on God.

I blame the Muslims, she cried. If we had all stayed in Lahore, you would have married a prince!

Blame the Mahatma, I shot back. Prakash would have been proud of me.

No! she cried, throwing her hands over her ears. God, maybe; the Mahatma, never.

A houseful of widows, that's what my son's house has become! she wailed. House of Sorrows! House of Ill Fortune!

Hari-prar arranged my illegal documents. It took him months, many trips to Chandigarh and Delhi, and cost me everything Prakash had saved. My passport name, officially, was Jyoti Vijh. My date of birth made me safely nineteen years old. "Otherwise, problems," said the travel advisers. All over Punjab "travel agents" are willing to advise. The longest line between two points is the least detected.

15

THERE are national airlines flying the world that do not appear in any directory. There are charters who've lost their way and now just fly, improvising crews and destinations. They serve no food, no beverages. Their crews often look abused. There is a shadow world of aircraft permanently aloft that share air lanes and radio frequencies with Pan Am and British Air and Air-India, portaging people who coexist with tourists and businessmen. But we are refugees and mercenaries and guest workers; you see us sleeping in airport lounges; you watch us unwrapping the last of our native foods, unrolling our prayer rugs, reading our holy books, taking out for the hundredth time an aerogram promising a job or space to sleep, a newspaper in our language, a photo of happier times, a passport, a visa, a *laissez-passer.*

We are the outcasts and deportees, strange pilgrims visiting outlandish shrines, landing at the end of tarmacs, ferried in old army trucks where we are roughly handled and taken to roped-off corners of waiting rooms where surly, barely wakened customs guards await their bribe. We are dressed in shreds of national costumes, out of season, the wilted plumage of intercontinental vagabondage. We ask only one thing: to be allowed to land; to pass through; to continue. We sneak a look at the big departure board, the one the tourists use. Our cities are there, too, our destinations are so close! But not yet, not so directly. We must sneak in, land by night in little-used strips. For us, back behind the rope in the corner of the waiting room, there is only a slate and someone who remembers to write in chalk, DELAYED, or TO BE ANNOUNCED, or OUT OF SERVICE. We take another of our precious dollars or Swiss francs and give it to a trustworthy-looking boy and say, "Bring me tea, an orange, bread."

What country? What continent? We pass through wars, through plagues. I am hungry for news, but the discarded papers are in characters or languages I cannot read.

The zigzag route is straightest.

I phantom my way through three continents. The small airports in the Middle East lit by oil fires and gas flares, the waiting rooms in Sudan with locusts banging on the glass, landing always in the smaller cities, the disused airfields.

On the first leg of my odyssey, I sit between a Filipina

nurse and a Tamil auto mechanic both on their way to Bahrain. I walk my swollen feet up and down the aisles of our 747. Whole peoples are on the move! The Filipina says, "The pay's great but I wish Bahrainis weren't Muslims." She shows me her St. Christopher medal on a blue sodality ribbon under her blouse. The Sri Lankan Tamil likes Muslims; he's not much taken with Buddhists and Christians. I keep my sandalwood Ganpati hidden in my purse, a god with an elephant trunk to uproot anything in my path.

I sit with missionaries, with the deported, with Australian students who've fallen somehow into the same loop of desperation, which is for them adventure. "Look," says one, "you'd love Owstrylia. Perth's just the plyce for you. Whatchu sye?" Hollow-eyed Muslim men in fur caps and woolen jackets, faces unshaven, make long-winded advances in Farsi and Pashto, elegant ghazals learned for the occasion, ripe with moons and figs and spurting fountains, then try out their broken Urdu when they guess I'm Indian.

In the soundproofed and windowless back room of an Indische Speishalle in Hamburg I watch on a tiny color television set the first of many wonders in the West, with cheering Arabs and Africans, the Hamburg Hummels cream the opposition. A Ugandan lifts his Mickey Mouse T-shirt to show off his flesh wounds. "When the American visa bastards turned me down, I tried to kill myself." Later, in suburban Blankenese, the *Polizei* pull the Ugandan and me off a train and ask to see our travel documents. I hand over my forged, expensive passport. The *Polizei* scrutinize my inscrutables, then let me go. The Ugandan twitches and stammers. The flesh wound bleeds into Mickey Mouse as he scuffles. On the train I weep at the beauty of the visa stamps Hari-prar has bought me. I feel renewed, the recipient of an organ transplant.

In Amsterdam a railway porter, a Surinamese Indian who speaks a little bit of Hindi, puts me in touch with the captain of a trawler who cargoes contraband into Paramaribo, then outward to the States.

16

O<small>N</small> the trawler out of Europe we slept in tiered bunks. In the New World, on a shrimper out of Grand Cayman called *The Gulf Shuttle*, four of us bound for the Gulf Coast of Florida slept under the tarp. You learn to roll with the waves and hold the vomit in.

Dayrise.

Gold gulls straddled topaz waves. Lapis fish leaped toward coral clouds. Some days the ocean was as stocked and still as an aquarium.

Nights, Half-Face, our captain, lullabyed us with his Willie Nelson tapes. Half-Face had lost an eye and ear and most of his cheek in a paddy field in Vietnam. Kingsland, a Jamaican, knew the story, because Half-Face was famous in the west Caribbean. Half-Face was a demolitions expert before he became a sea captain. When I passed that on to Little Clyde, an anxious Belizian, he worried, "We got ourssels a clumsy mon! You waitn see, we end up domped in dat goddom ocean!"

On his last crossing, Little Clyde fell into vigilante hands in Texas. "Dey cotched dat boy like a fish," Kingsland said, "and dey cotted him just like dey do fish. We find him like fish, guts dryin in de sun. Why de world go de way it do, girl?"

I didn't console Kingsland with Vedic slokas about fish and fishermen. He needed to gorge his paranoia. Little Clyde's vigilantes had ways: wet mattresses, electric cattle prods, quart bottles of cola. What was the bottle of cola for? He said that first the vigilantes forced the Coke up Little Clyde's nose. "Den dey shov de empty bottle up his arsehole, girl."

Little Clyde smiled. "Dis time I do it right, mon."

The woman from Mauritius, the only other woman on the boat, and mostly Indian, to look at, cried when she heard the story about Little Clyde and the vigilantes. She was a fervent Catholic with a French accent. She cried for her father, who would turn in his grave if he knew that she was subjected to words like "arsehole." In Port Louis she had studied in a convent school. I disappointed her. To her I was a coarse, common girl, a peasant. She kept herself sane singing Gilbert and Sullivan songs, which she said were British. Kingsland also knew Gilbert and Sullivan. I'd never heard of them. I was born into India's near-middle age. British things were gone, and in our village they'd never even arrived.

One evening Half-Face lectured us on deck about some dos and don'ts. He said, "Listen up. Here's the emergency drill. Three blasts of the whistle and you hit the water. *Comprende?*"

The dead dog in the river never seemed so close. I smelled softening flesh.

"After landfall, if the Border Patrol picks you up and hauls your ass off to the detention center, you don't know us. You never sailed *The Gulf Shuttle*. You fucking walked on water, okay?"

The Mauritian wept delicately into a handkerchief. I asked her why she was with us, with her education and soft hands, but she never answered. No work, dead parents, bad marriage, and you end up on a shrimper in the Gulf, under a tarp. You end up bait-fish, Kingsland said.

"What's the problem, hon?" Half-Face asked. "I don't see the problem." To the rest of us he said, "You need accommodations, we got accommodations. It'll cost you, but we got them. You need transportation, we'll truck you anywhere you want."

Kingsland whispered to me, "Don't truss dat mon, no way." Then he slipped a surprise farewell present into my palm. I felt the nicked handle butt of a knife, not much bigger than the penknives that my brothers had whittled sticks with to play their danda goli games. "You con count on dat at least, when de end of de world come in."

*   *   *

Deeper into the night, Half-Face's crew took down the tarp tent. Their flashlights bobbed in blackness. I smelled the unrinsed water of a distant shore. Then suddenly in the pinkening black of pre-dawn, America caromed off the horizon.

The first thing I saw were the two cones of a nuclear plant, and smoke spreading from them in complicated but seemingly purposeful patterns, edges lit by the rising sun, like a gray, intricate map of an unexplored island continent, against the pale unscratched blue of the sky. I waded through Eden's waste: plastic bottles, floating oranges, boards, sodden boxes, white and green plastic sacks tied shut but picked open by birds and pulled apart by crabs.

In a clearing by the cove, white men with sneering faces waited in panel trucks with engines running to transport us to points south and north. Little Clyde and Kingsland shook clean slacks, shirts, leather shoes out of plastic bags and changed into them. Their old clothes were balled up and tossed into the ocean. Kingsland even had a pack of Fresh-Ups on him. His well-fleshed face glistened clean as he climbed into a truck. I still had Prakash's heavy suitcase.

Du also remembers clothes lying flat on the beach, as though the people inside had been zapped by aliens. I've told him this much of my arrival. The assholes.

* * *

The better-heeled got in panel trucks. Little Clyde got in the rusting trunk of a sedan. The Mauritian girl got put in the back seat. We didn't wave.

I dragged my suitcase up the sandy trail. Crabs scuttled underfoot.

"What, no takers for you?" Half-Face honked at me from a great boat of a car.

I kept walking.

He stopped the car and got out. He put his hand over mine on the handle of the suitcase and waited for me to withdraw it. Then he picked up the suitcase and slung it into the back seat of the car. "Get in," he said. He fixed me with his dead eye and said, "There's some bad fellows up yonder. Best you and me keep us a little company."

17

I WONDER if Bud even sees the America I do. We pass half-built, half-deserted cinder-block structures at the edge of town, with mud-spattered deserted cars parked in an uncleared lot, and I wonder, Who's inside? What are they doing? Who's hiding? Empty swimming pools and plywood panels in the window frames grip my guts. And Bud frowns because unproductive projects give him pain. He says, "Wonder who handled their financing."

My first night in America was spent in a motel with plywood over its windows, its pool bottomed with garbage sacks, and grass growing in its parking lot.

Half-Face whisked me inland off the keys, deep into pine and Sabal palm country, off narrow roads with scooped-out ditches on either side. It felt as if we were driving on the tops of dikes, with fields of swamp grass between us and the walls of leggy trees. The landscape was not unfamiliar: monsoon season in Punjab.

No tourist would ever stay at the Flamingo Court. The neon bird was browned out, the only lights that worked blazed a big red NO in front of VACANCY. Plywood panels didn't matter much. I'd grown up sleeping four sisters to a bamboo mat on a cold adobe floor. I was seventeen years old. Why shouldn't I have been taken in by the splendors of an abandoned motel?

Half-Face looked at me, amused. "So, you don't mind ending up here with me instead of in the back of a cattle truck?" Six of one, he said, half dozen the other. He leaned across my lap to unlock the door on my side. The mangled side of his face came at me, like a bat in a night-black forest. I stepped out of the car, fast.

Ours seemed to be the only sedan in the parking lot. The rest were panel trucks and pickups. A cabless semi all atilt was parallel-parked by the chain-link fence in the back of the motel. The abandoned semi was a bunkhouse, too, for cut-rate undocumenteds. Short, dark-skinned, black-haired women sat outside it, tending a fire. Beyond the fence was woodsy blackness.

Someone called to Half-Face from the ground-floor porch of the motel. It sounded like "Baba!"

In the sour yellow light of the porch, I made out a fat black man in a T-shirt and jeans. "No way you goin stuff one more body into 201, Bubba. You caint stuff even one mo mouse into dat room!"

"Wasn't plannin on it anyhow, Lonzell," Half-Face snorted. "This'n here's my own special lookout. Me'n her's been traveling a long ways together." He hefted my bag up the pink spiraling stairs that could have been straight out of an Amitav Bhacchan film set.

"How come you have an Indian name?" I asked as I spiraled up just behind him.

"Come again?"

"The man called you Baba."

Half-Face looked lost for a second. Then he grinned on his good side. "You better reset your ears, honey. It's Bubba," he said. "Bubba ain't no Indian name, no way. In the nigger-shipping bizness we don't bother with last names."

He strode down the entire length of the second-floor porch; I kept up as slowly as I dared. What was fated to happen would happen. My mission, thank God, was nearly over. Half-Face set my bag down in front of the door to the corner room. "What would a little girl like you be needing with such a heavy bag?"

He unlocked the door and shoved the bag over the threshold. "Note," he said, "you are entering because you want to. No coercion involved." He faced me, hands at his side, palms up. "Haven't I been a perfect gentleman? Offering a ride, carrying your bag? Well?"

"Yes," I admitted. "Thank you for everything."

"What do I get?" I extended my hand and he nearly ripped it off, pulling me into the room. His leg flew waist-high in a show-offy kick and the door thumped closed. He grabbed me and pulled me against him and started kissing.

I could feel the dead half-mouth against mine, and the one glass eye staring down.

"What's your problem, cold fish? I thought you'd be different from the others. A spark, you know?" I wiped my mouth.

"I saw you carrying on with that jigaboo Jamaican. You don't like white men, that it?" He strutted around the room—his office, he called it, his home away from home. There were framed pictures on the dresser, men in T-shirts with caps on, a trophy with a man crouching and holding a ball no larger than a cardamon pod. Mrs. Half-Face and maybe some children. A pair of shoes with the number 12 stamped on the back.

"Well, I reckon we'll have time to get used to each other. Kind of adjust and get comfy, you know?" He turned on the air conditioner, the TV, the radio, the bathroom light-and-fan combination. "See, see? Deluxe stuff."

I said, "My husband is a genius at repairing televisions."

"Is he, now. That's very interesting. Give him a call, tell him to come over and watch." He started laughing, great croupy wheezes, and pulled me to him for another kiss. "Look, just don't fuck with me. I been to Asia and it's the armpit of the universe." He dragged me to the television and pressed my forehead against the screen. Then he brought my head back and slammed it against the set, again and again. "Don't tell me you ever *seen* a television set. Don't lie to me about no husbands and no television and we'll get along real good. I got things I can do for you and you got something you can do for me, and I got lots of other things I can do *to* you, understand?"

There was a small crack on the television screen. "Now look and see what you done to my television. You sorry, or what?" I reached for my forehead, no blood. I squeezed my eyes shut and felt my scar tightening, and the heat from the screen on my swelling.

I remembered Prakash, sitting cross-legged on our bed under the fan as he repaired Mrs. Jagtiani's VCR and Mr. Jagtiani's old German shaver. His hand on mine, directing the tweezers, "There! Perfect!" and sighing, "That bloodsucker Sindhi is destroying my spirit."

I started to cry.

He pulled me off the floor and dropped me on the bed. "Okay, baby, we're going to keep this simple. I got one use for you, and you got no use for me, and you know what? That don't bother me at all. In fact, it's sort of a turn-on." He started undoing his belt. "I don't think you like me much, do you?" He turned his bad side to me. "This sorta makes you sick, don't it? You're afraid I'm going to rub the scars all over your pretty little face, aren't you?"

He looked at me, and at the suitcase, then he rubbed his jaw, a man with too many options. He hefted the bag onto the bed and unsnapped the catches. Out came my sandal-wood Ganpati. He propped it up against a picture on the dresser. He noticed my photo album and picked it up. Pictures of Prakash and of Pitaji, wrapped in an old sari. He flipped through them all, raising an eyebrow at pictures of me in a sari, leaning on the old Bajaj. Some clothes. At the bottom, the blue suit, unworn, still folded with its BABUR ALI/MASTER TAILOR/JULLUNDHAR on the sleeve. He got a kick out of this, slipping on the jacket, only to find that he couldn't button it or move his arms.

"Who's this for?" he demanded. "A kid?"

"It is my husband's," I said.

"Kind of a scrawny little bastard, ain't he?" He laughed and dropped the jacket back in the suitcase. "You made me carry this shit up here? You carried all this shit halfway around the world? You crazy or what? Travel light, sweetheart, always travel light. If you hadn't been carrying this bag, you wouldn't be in the deep shit now, you know that? Ever think of that? 'Course, I'm not objecting."

"I promised," I said. "It is my mission to bring my husband's suit to America. I am taking it to his school and burning it where we were going to live."

"Yeah, where?"

"Tam-pah," I said.

"Well, shit, that's not far at all. I'll drive you down there in the morning. Wouldn't burn it, though, might seem a little suspicious." He laughed the wracking series that ended in spit.

"Christ," he said. "Getting your ass kicked halfway around the world just to burn a suit. I never heard such a fool notion."

He laughed again, ending in the cough. We are all put on this earth for a purpose, Mataji would have said. All acts are connected. For every monster there is a hero. For every hero, a monster. He closed the suitcase and laid it on the floor.

"As I was saying." He laughed. "Just you keep it coming and I'm your meal ticket outta here. Give me any grief and you're dead meat."

He went into the bathroom and came out with a glass of something in his hand. He sloshed almost all of it down in one long gulp before dropping heavily back on the bed. I watched him drink. He had slack, flabby, inefficient lips.

"Water," I said. "Water would taste very good."

He stayed on the bed. "You staring for a reason?" I asked for water again. I wanted him out of the room. "You know what's coming, and there ain't nobody here to help you, so my advice is lie back and enjoy it. Hell, you'll probably like it. I don't get many complaints."

"My husband was killed," I said. "Please don't do anything to me."

He pulled the drawstring of my salwar pants. "I'm real sorry, but I didn't do it, lady. Like I said, don't give me grief."

He turned his back and pulled down his pants. "You better be getting out of that shirt."

"He died in my arms. He's here, you know."

Half-Face turned. "Sure he is. In the closet, right? I told you about the shirt."

"He's in this room."

"Okay, I'll buy that. You're a grieving widow. But you're also one prime little piece, and where I come from, that cancels out."

Half-Face stood, totally naked. He was monstrously erect. Prakash had always been so concerned for me. He was afraid of youthful pregnancy, of children bearing children. He talked to me of muscles tearing, of the girl's body only *looking* mature, no matter what the rituals, the feudalisms, said. For the first time in my life I understood what evil was about. It was about not being human. Half-Face was from an underworld of evil. It was a very simple, very clear perception, a moment of truth, the kind of understanding that I have heard comes at the moment of death. I had faced death twice before, and cheated it.

Yama will not sneak up on me.

"I want water, please."

"Yeah, okay. You'll get your water." He went to the bathroom for me, and when he came back, the glass of water was brown and smelled of the liquor on his breath. He pulled off the puffy panties from Europe I'd been wearing.

He stared. His hands were trembling and then he whooped, "Oh, God!" and tried to kiss me, but he was all hands and face in motion. I twisted, only delaying the inevitable, making it worse perhaps, more forced, more violent. I tried to keep my eyes on Ganpati and prayed for the strength to survive, long enough to kill myself.

"Use a drink?" He lay back beside me, one thick arm over me, the other one with the glass. "I must use the bathroom," I said, and he let me up. I picked my pants up off the floor and tried to be modest. He balled up my shirt and put it under his head, a second pillow.

"Get yourself cleaned up, but don't take all night," he

shouted. "Second time's the sweetest." He seemed to find it amusing. I turned on the shower, making it hot. With water pelting the shower curtain, I vomited. Then I showered. I had never used a Western shower, standing instead of squatting, with automatic hot water coming hard from a nozzle instead of cool water from a hand-dipped pitcher. It seemed like a miracle, that even here in a place that looked deserted, a place like a madhouse or a prison, where the most hideous crimes took place, the water should be hot, the tiles and porcelain should be clean, without smells, without bugs. It was a place that permitted a kind of purity.

I determined to clean my body as it had never been cleaned, with the small wrapped bar of soap, and to purify my soul with all the prayers I could remember from my father's and my husband's cremations. This would be a fitting place to die. I had left my earthly body and would soon be joining their souls.

The bathroom steamed like a smokehouse. I reached into the pocket of my salwar for Kingsland's knife. Until the moment that I held its short, sharp blade to my throat I had not thought of any conclusion but the obvious one: to balance my defilement with my death. I could not see myself in the steamed-up mirror—only a dark shadow in the center of the glass. I could not see, as I had wanted to, an arm reaching to the neck, the swift slice, the end of my mission.

It was the murkiness of the mirror and a sudden sense of mission that stopped me. What if my mission was not yet over? I didn't *feel* the passionate embrace of Lord Yama that could turn a kerosene flame into a lover's caress. I could not let my personal dishonor disrupt my mission. There would be plenty of time to die; I had not yet burned my husband's suit. I had not stood under the palm trees of the college campus.

I extended my tongue, and sliced it. Hot blood dripped immediately in the sink.

I had planned it all so perfectly. To lay out the suit, to fill it with twigs and papers. To light it, then to lie upon it in the white cotton sari I had brought from home.

I put on my pants and wrapped myself in the towel for the iciness outside. He was, as I had hoped, asleep in his total nakedness, hands clasped peacefully around the glass of half-drunk whiskey balanced on his chest. I drew close to the side of the bed, next to the nightstand, where I could study the good side of his face. My mouth had filled with blood. I could feel it on my chin.

I began to shiver. The blade need not be long, only sharp, and my hand not strong, only quick. His eyes fluttered open even before I felt the metal touch his throat, and his smile and panic were nearly instantaneous. I wanted that moment when he saw me above him as he had last seen me, naked, but now with my mouth open, pouring blood, my red tongue out. I wanted him to open his mouth and start to reach, I wanted that extra hundredth of a second when the blade bit deeper than any insect, when I jumped back as he jerked forward, slapping at his neck while blood, ribbons of bright blood, rushed between his fingers.

He got his legs over the side of the bed, he stood and staggered, and with each stagger new spatter marks gushed against the walls. He kept trying to stop the blood, but the cut was small and he couldn't find where so much blood, his blood, was coming from. His hands kept slipping, and finally he fell to his knees at the foot of the bed. I dragged the suitcase to the farthest end of the room. He tried to rise and couldn't. I pulled the bedspread off the bed and threw it over him and then began stabbing wildly through the cloth, as the human form beneath it grew smaller and stiller.

No one to call to, no one to disturb us. Just me and the man who had raped me, the man I had murdered. The room looked like a slaughterhouse. Blood had congealed on my hands, my chin, my breasts. What a monstrous thing, what an infinitesimal thing, is the taking of a human life; for the second time in three months, I was in a room with a *slain* man, my body bloodied. I was walking death. Death incarnate.

This time, my response was calm. I went back to the shower and purified myself once again. I gargled blood and cold water until the bleeding stopped. I tried to speak, but my tongue burned and refused to bend. Then I opened the suitcase and changed into my last clean salwar-kameez.

I stuffed the suitcase with my dishonored old clothes. The widow's white sari and Prakash's suit remained. I took out a blue-jean jacket bought for me in Delhi by my brothers. There were booklets of matches everywhere; I helped myself. And then I remembered something that surprises me to this day: I remembered the hateful police inspector in Jullundhar, his reports to us of fingerprint evidence on the bomb fragments. I'd been impressed, and now I remembered. I went back to the bathroom and wiped the sink and shower taps.

I took the suitcase with me. Out to the porch, down the spiral stairs. It was a loud, bug-infested night; frogs chorused from a nearby swamp. Fireflies winked before me like lights from anchored trawlers in a choppy sea.

Around back, there were rusty metal trash bins, punched with holes for better ventilation. I laid the suitcase inside one and lit it from the bottom. It sputtered and flared. The outside melted, but then the cotton and wool ignited.

I said my prayers for the dead, clutching my Ganpati. I thought, The pitcher is broken. Lord Yama, who had wanted me, who had courted me, and whom I'd flirted with on the long trip over, had now deserted me.

I had not given even a day's survival in America a single thought. This was the place I had chosen to die, on the first day if possible. I would land, find Tampah, walking there if necessary, find the college grounds and check it against the brochure photo. Under the very tree where two Indian boys and two Chinese girls were pictured, smiling, I had dreamed of arranging the suit and twigs. The vision of lying serenely on a bed of fire under palm trees in my white sari had motivated all the weeks of sleepless, half-starved passage, the numbed surrender to various men for the reward of an orange, a blanket, a slice of cheese. I had protected this sari, and Prakash's suit, through it all. Then he had touched it. He had put on the suit, touched my sari, my photographs and Ganpati.

My body was merely the shell, soon to be discarded. Then I could be reborn, debts and sins all paid for.

If he had only killed me. If he had only left my mission alone. He made me say it, he laughed at it.

Suddenly death was being denied.

I buttoned up the jacket and sat by the fire. With the first streaks of dawn, my first full American day, I walked out the front drive of the motel to the highway and began my journey, traveling light.

18

At the University Club over in Dalton, the woman who's invited me to lunch says, pressing her fingertips lightly on my arm, "I've been wanting to make this call to you for so long! Then finally yesterday I said, What the hell, I'll call, and if she doesn't want to meet me, all she can say is no."

It is not likely that I would have refused a professor's request. I'd cashed checks for her at the bank and thought her a perfectly reasonable, attractive, soft-spoken, mid-fortyish professional woman.

Her name is Mary Webb, Dr. Mary Webb, with no husband and a big balance listed on her bank records, and she teaches sociology or social work. In the bank, she'd always seemed circumspect and sober, but here she's alternately intense and extroverted, with a lime-green barrette in her bobbed hair, glasses rimmed in red plastic, and orange ankle socks. The socks are dyed the orange of Indian swamis' robes. She does not look like a madwoman.

"I'm glad you called," I say. What can I say? I look around the small dining room, three tables of ten people each. More women than men. I'm the youngest by at least twenty years. I've already been asked what I am studying. I say, "I'm honored to be with all these learned people." She laughs harshly. I assume all the men and women wielding forks are scholars, more masterly than poor Masterji. I, a dropout from a village school. America, America!

She leans close and confides, "The things that really matter to me I can't share with anyone outside the group. This is my group. You must know how it is. Then I saw you in the bank, and right away I had this frisson. I knew I could talk to you."

"About what?" Suspicion must tinge my voice.

She makes sure the waiter is out of hearing range before she continues. "If I say the word 'channeling,' what do you think of?"

"Digging?" I say.

"Oh, marvelous. Exactly! *Digging.*" The extrovert beams; then intensity takes over. She barely whispers.

"Digging for what, do you suppose?"

I don't want to disappoint her. I whisper back, because something in the conspiracy compels it, "Bodies?"

She throws her hands up in delight. "Oh, you've got it! I just knew you would."

Mary Webb is telling me about her out-of-body experiences. They are visceral revelations about her pre-life. They used to come upon her out of the blue, in the middle of grading papers maybe, or while shaking herself a margarita (her only vice, this time around), but now she's learning to make them happen by going to a guru who runs a bimonthly group.

In her last fully retrievable life she was a man. Her gaze is steady; apparently I haven't reacted. A black man. She leans closer. Not an American, no, an *Australian* black man, an Aborigine. I still haven't flinched, though I'm desperately trying to process the incongruity. When she's channeling, she speaks the tribal language perfectly, of course, and even now she remembers a few word-clots. She renames the plates, table, chairs in a strangely glottal series of articulated gulps. "Of course, we don't have plates. We have bowls made out of skulls and gourds. I'm just approximating. Table, as well. Same with chair. I'm really just giving you verbs for sitting, eating, etc."

She's been unable to have a conversation with an Aborigine anywhere in Iowa, though not for lack of searching. One Australian in the music department has listened to a few sentences from her and said it *sounded* Abo to him.

In her most recent adventure, she is closing in on a giant kangaroo—an extinct species, incidentally, the size of a bounding bison—she can taste the meat. She might be the only person in Iowa with such vivid nostalgia for kangaroo flesh. She/he can anticipate the sexual gratitude of his/her wife, and the admiration of the children—she knows the names of all four, three boys and a girl (do I want to hear them?)—waiting for him/her back in their camp.

"Do they, you, live in tents?" I ask. It's my first chance to break in.

"Actually, a cave. Face of a cliff, overlooking a vast, flat plain." A few trees, some water holes. White men haven't arrived yet, it's pre-Edenic. It seems that her lives have jumped a groove, like a record arm that gets bumped, and she's landed up *there* at the dawn of her immortal soul's mutable, genetic journey, with no knowledge of the thousands of other lives she must have led in between. The other lives are just fragmentary. She has been in many wars, wandered in many forests, borne many children.

Her face *is* transformed as she tells me. Her voice drops, there is a slight Australian diction to her description. "My forearms thickened and muscled. It was so wonderful and weird. My arm and a giant boomerang were one long, curved line. When I let it go, it felt better than an orgasm."

"Theoretically, I believe in reincarnation," I say. I am astounded by all this, the American need to make intuition so tangible, to *possess* a vision so privately.

Mary Webb's guru is a thirty-six-year-old woman who calls herself Ma Leela. "She needed to visit the earth, so she made contact with a woman who'd made up her mind to commit suicide in Medicine Hat, Alberta. This other woman was a battered wife, and she was severely depressed and there was no talking her out of the suicide. So Ma Leela said, If you are sure you are going to go through with vacating your body, I'd like to take it over."

I ask Mary Webb how Ma Leela knew that a body was about to be vacated in Alberta, and she explains that in Ma Leela's natural sphere there is a data bank of bodyflow.

"We believe the body is like a revolving door. So she split her body. The doctors thought they'd saved her by pumping her stomach clean of Seconal, but the person they released from the hospital was Ma Leela. Now Ma Leela is doing her healing all over the Midwest and the Northwest." She looks around the room, expansively. "We're all in Ma Leela's group."

My face must have a funny look, because Mary Webb manages to say, before the waiter comes to our table, "This can't be new or bizarre to you. Don't you Hindus keep revisiting the world?"

The waiter has HI, I'M DUANE pinned on his white shirt. I order pork chops, thinking any pork sale is good for Darrel and Elsa County. Mary Webb says, "I thought you'd be vegetarian," and orders something called Salade au Printemps. When the waiter leaves, I tell her that yes, I am sure that I have been reborn several times, and that yes, some lives I can recall vividly.

I am moved by Mary Webb's story. What if the human soul is eternal—the swamis say of it, fires cannot burn it, water cannot drown it, winds cannot bend it—what if it is like a giant long-playing record with millions of tracks, each of them a complete circle with only one diamond-sharp microscopic link to the next life, and the next, and only God to hear it all?

I do believe that. And I do believe that extraordinary events can jar the needle arm, jump tracks, rip across incarnations, and deposit a life into a groove that was not prepared to receive it.

I should never have been Jane Ripplemeyer of Baden, Iowa. I should have lived and died in that feudal village, perhaps making a monumental leap to modern Jullundhar. When Jyoti's future was blocked after the death of Prakash, Lord Yama should have taken her.

"Yes," I say, "I do believe you. We do keep revisiting the world. I have also traveled in time and space. It is possible."

Jyoti of Hasnapur was not Jasmine, Duff's day mummy and Taylor and Wylie's *au pair* in Manhattan; *that* Jasmine isn't *this* Jane Ripplemeyer having lunch with Mary Webb at the University Club today. And which of us is the undetected murderer of a half-faced monster, which of us has held a dying husband, which of us was raped and raped and raped in boats and cars and motel rooms?

I found Taylor and Wylie Hayes through Lillian Gordon, a kind Quaker lady who rescued me from a dirt trail about three miles east of Fowlers Key, Florida. In my fake American jacket, salwar-kameez, and rhinestoned

Jullundhari sandals, with only a purse, Ganpati, and forged documents, I had walked out of an overpopulated, deserted motel and followed a highway headed north; that's all I knew. In India, I would have come upon at least a village or two, but in Florida there was only the occasional country store or trailer park. I hadn't a penny.

Honoring all prescriptions for a purified body, anticipating only release from this world, I had not eaten in two days. I had taken no water, especially not in the glass that Half-Face offered.

Around noon, I could go no farther. My swollen, festering tongue was an agony, nearly choking me. A sandy trail tunneled through a distant row of mossy trees. Battered trucks full of produce kept pulling out. More trucks, filled with laborers, turned in. It was as though I'd never left India. After a few minutes, a station wagon driven by a lone woman followed. Fields on either side of the highway were dense with tomatoes, eggplants, and okra (still aubergines and ladies' fingers in Masterji's English). I had traveled the world without ever leaving the familiar crops of Punjab. Thinking I was among farmers, that I might find food, water, and work, I decided to follow the trail.

Trash cans lined one edge of the clearing. So much trash in America! Bony dogs leaped and snarled at the end of short chains. Mangy hens scuttled in and out of dried-out tire ruts. Short, thick, dark-skinned men with vaguely Asian features—Nepalese, I thought at the time, Gurkhas; can this torture all be a dream? where have I come to?—

shadowed the windows and doorways of an old barracks, and a wingless parrot hopped on a rusty bar.

A boy whistled at me from behind a tree. I couldn't tell his age. He had a child's body: fat stomach and thin legs with crusting sores, but a wrinkled, cynical face. I had been in America nearly a day and had yet to see an "American" face. He carried a plastic Uzi, not that different from the hardware of the Khalsa Lions, and he had the Uzi pointed at me. He did impressive sound effects, too. *Kssss! Kssss!*

"Water," I tried to say. "Pump." Blood still drained from my mouth.

The boy dropped down into a sniper's crouch and sprayed me one more time.

I made a pumping, drinking gesture.

At the far end of the clearing, by the trash cans, a man was teaching two others to drive a low-sprung old sedan. I waved my hands over my head, then pointed to my mouth. "Wah-huh!" I shouted at them. The man behind the steering wheel got out of the sedan. He mimicked the way I talked and walked. The boy and all three men laughed.

The driver of the sedan kicked a cola can and sent it clanking toward me. "No work!" he snapped. "This Kanjobal crew. Vamoose! Fuck off! Get lost!"

At that moment, an old white lady came out of the barracks. She wore a wide-brimmed straw hat, dark glasses, a T-shirt, and black pants. She must have been seventy. From the doorway she called, "Carlos! How dare you speak to a young lady in such a despicable fashion. She asked for water—well, get her water, man!"

She came to me and put her hands on my shoulders. "Child! What is it? You're trembling." She led me to the stairs and sat me down on the middle one. "What in God's name is this country coming to!" She stood and clapped her hands and shouted out a series of names or commands in a rapid language. Soon, a woman appeared with food on a paper plate and a plastic fork. It was the first hot, prepared food I'd had in over a month. But when I laid a forkful of it on my tongue, I nearly passed out with pain. The woman walked me to her car.

"My name is Lillian Gordon," she said. "I won't ask yours because it's probably a fake. *This* I take it—she was feeling my kameez—isn't Guatemalan, is it? Are we talking India here? Punjab? Are you Sikh?"

I managed only to shake my head vigorously, no. "Hin—du," I finally said.

"Lord. Well, there's nothing we can do here, is there? And I suppose those chappies from the INS would leap at the sight of you in those sandals." She motioned me to get in the station wagon.

Lillian Gordon took me home with her. Home was a wooden house on stilts on blackish swampy ground. But over there, she said, over the black muck and just beyond a fringe of bent Sabal palms, was the Gulf. I got her older daughter's bedroom. Framed, amateurish photos lined the walls. "Kate took those in high school," Lillian said. Sunsets on the beach, a dog. Pretty, but not special. In college she'd come back one summer and shot in a migrant-worker camp. Five years later she'd done work with the Kanjobals in Florida, the basis of a book that had won a prize. Lillian showed me the book. The pictures brought back such memories of Hasnapur, I wept. That daughter now lived in New York and was a professional photographer. Another daughter was in Guatemala working with Kanjobal Indians. Three Kanjobal women slept in bunk beds in that daughter's room.

I didn't tell Mrs. Gordon what she'd rescued me from. In some fundamental way, she didn't care. I was no threat, and I was in need. The world's misery was a challenge to her ingenuity. She brought a doctor in to sew my tongue. The Kanjobal women in her house had all lost their husbands and children to an army massacre. She forbade all discussion of it. She had a low tolerance for reminiscence, bitterness or nostalgia. Let the past make you wary, by all means. But do not let it deform you. Had I said, "I murdered a man last night," she might have said, "I'm sure you had an excellent reason. Next time, please, less salt in the eggplant." If I had said, "He raped me," she certainly would have squinted sympathetically, then said, "You're not the first and you won't be the last. Will you be needing an abortion?" She wasn't a missionary dispensing new visions and stamping out the old; she was a facilitator who made possible the lives of absolute *ordinariness* that we ached for.

I was lucky, she said, that India had once been a British colony. Can you imagine being stuck with a language like Dutch or Portuguese? "Look at these poor Kanjobal—they barely speak Spanish!" Lillian, of course, had taught herself Kanjobal. She felt it was the least she could do.

She gave me her daughter's high-school clothes: blouses with Peter Pan collars, maxi skirts, T-shirts with washed-out pictures, sweaters, cords, and loafers. But beware the shoes, she said, shoes are the biggest giveaway. Undocumented aliens wear boxy shoes with ambitious heels. She opened her thumb and index finger a good six inches, like a crocodile's mouth.

Suddenly it all came back: Jullundhar, Prakash, a day just before the end, at Bata Shoes. An image triggered the tears, the screams. The Kanjobal women left the room; Lillian stayed with me, brewing tea.

Prakash in his peach-colored bell-bottomed slacks, kicking off his chappals and asking to see their best "Western" burra sahib leather shoes. Oh, he looked so tall, so proud, lifted in those shoes that gleamed like oiled hair in their boxy brilliance.

"See how tall I am, Jasmine?"

"Put these things away," he said to me back in the apartment. "No more chappals for me." I felt love like a razor slash across my eyes and tongue, and now with a touch of shame.

"My daughter calls them Third World heels," Lillian said, laughed, after the tea had calmed me down. Walk American, she exhorted me, and she showed me how. I worked hard on the walk and deportment. Within a week she said I'd lost my shy sidle. She said I walked like one of those Trinidad Indian girls, all thrust and cheekiness. She meant it as a compliment.

"Tone it down, girl!" She clapped as I took a turn between the kitchen and bath. I checked myself in the mirror, shocked at the transformation. Jazzy in a T-shirt, tight cords, and running shoes. I couldn't tell if with the Hasnapuri sidle I'd also abandoned my Hasnapuri modesty.

We drove into a mall in Clearwater for the test. Time to try out my American talk and walk. Lillian called me "Jazzy." In one of the department stores I saw my first revolving door. How could something be always open and at the same time always closed? She had me try out my first escalator. How could something be always moving and always still?

At the bottom of the escalator she said, "They pick up dark people like you who're afraid to get on or off." I shut my eyes and stepped forward and kept my eyes closed all the way to the top. I waited for the hairy arm of the law to haul me in. Instead, Lillian said, "You pass, Jazzy." She gave me two dollars. "Now, how about buying me a Dairy Queen?"

I remember Dairy Queen as my first true American food. How it soothed my still-raw tongue. I thought of it as healing food.

The Kanjobal women didn't speak any English. For them Lillian's small house on stilts must have felt like a safe garrison in hostile territory. At the time I felt a little bitter, nostalgic for their locked and companionable world. They showed me how to pat grainy tortilla dough into shape, and I showed them how to roll the thinnest, roundest chapatis. And Lillian taught us all to cook hamburgers and roasts, to clean toilets with cleansers that smelled sweeter than flowers, and to scrub pots and pans with pre-soaped balls of steel wool instead of ashes and lemon rinds, so we could hire ourselves out as domestics.

At the end of a week, Lillian said in her brisk, direct way at the breakfast table, "Jazzy, you don't strike me as a picker or a domestic." The Kanjobal women looked at her intently, nodding their heads as if they understood. "You're different from these others. I better put on my thinking cap and come up with something."

I said, "I want to go to New York. I have an address there." I showed her the back of Professor Devinder Vadhera's aerogram.

She read off the address. "Kissena Boulevard, Flushing," she repeated. "I suppose Queens isn't what it used to be."

She packed me a suitcase full of her daughter's old clothes that evening, and two days later she put me on a Greyhound bus. At the bus station she gave me her final tips. "Now remember, if you walk and talk American, they'll think you were born here. Most Americans can't imagine anything else." She penned a Manhattan address on the back of a blank check and slipped it to me. "But just in case you get picked up at the Port Authority—you never know how the Good Lord intends to test you—call my daughter. At least she'll be able to get you a lawyer."

And then she gave me a hug and a kiss. "Quite uncharacteristic," she said, "but impulsive and sincere. You're a very special case, my dear. I've written that to my daughter, so don't hesitate to call her."

19

B EFORE the courts busted her for harboring undocumenteds, *exploiting* them (the prosecution said) for free
cooking, cleaning, and yard work, Lillian used to send me
twenty dollars and a pair of hand-knitted pink wool slippers
every Christmas. She did the same for everyone she'd ever
helped. They would arrive care of her daughter, Kate
Gordon-Feldstein, the photographer and friend of Taylor
and Wylie. Lillian made certain that my name and address
never appeared in her files. I have three sets of identical
slippers. Once she learned a pattern, she never varied. I
treasure them as a devotee might a saint's relics.

I couldn't testify for her, given my own delicate status.
My anonymous letter of support was ruled inadmissible. I

wrote that she saved my life, after others had tried to end it. She represented to me the best in the American experience and the American character. She went to jail for refusing to name her contacts or disclose the names and addresses of the so-called army of illegal aliens she'd helped "dump" on the welfare rolls of America. In prison she got sick, and they pardoned the contempt charge to let her die at home.

About a year ago, Wylie wrote me out here in Iowa. She was trying to get her bosses interested in *An American Kind of Saint*, the Lillian Gordon story. She wondered if I would participate. Anonymously, yes. The project looked good for a few months. As the editor, maybe even the author, Wylie had public access to Kate and confidential access to me.

"We could get a made-for-TV movie out of it. Katharine Hepburn to star," she said. "Crusty and unvarnished, but with very good bones." Then the project crashed. The demographics weren't there. People were getting a little scared of immigrants and positively hostile to illegals.

Kate, the ironist, wrote me that she and her sister sold the house on stilts to a retired orthodontist from Tampa. For back taxes, he'd already picked up and remodeled a deserted motel down the road (the Flamingo Court, did I know it?), then he bought the barracks and the land around the Kanjobal settlement, and now, with Lillian's property, he was advertising a "Key West–style cottage," for people accustomed to "a slower, more gracious time." He's developing the whole area into something called Paradise Bay Complex: A Mixed-Use Vacation and Residence Community.

A sanctuary transformed into a hotel; hell turned into paradise—to me this seems very American. The brochure says that Paradise Bay is situated "just steps away from a private marina." Is this the scummy, collared cove bobbing with garbage sacks where Half-Face beached us? Now the new Flamingo Court Hotel is a ten-minute drive from a 2,400-foot airstrip. Goodbye, nigger shipping! Hello, America! New Half-Faces have found a more profitable product.

At Paradise Place, a one-bedroom unit with Gulf front, bath, and balcony costs $280 a night. That would be Kate's old room and mine. The Kanjobal women's room is described as having a "Gulf breeze." During our cut-rate residence with Lillian, we stayed away from the windows. We didn't check out the fishing promised in the brochure either. Pompano, grouper, cobia; trout, mackerel, redfish, flounder, mullet; blue crabs and stone crabs. I do remember flying fish striking the deck of *The Gulf Shuttle*, and crawling after them before they slithered overboard.

In the brochure, fit blond young couples charter fishing boats, play tennis, train binoculars on bald eagles and spoonbills, slather each other with sunscreen lotions.

It is by now only a passing wave of nausea, this response to the speed of transformation, the fluidity of American character and the American landscape. I feel at times like a stone hurtling through diaphanous mist, unable to grab hold, unable to slow myself, yet unwilling to abandon the ride I'm on. Down and down I go, where I'll stop, God only knows.

At ten in the morning on a Monday I arrived in New York City. There were scores of policemen swinging heavy nightsticks, but none of them pounced on me at the bottom of the escalator. They were, indeed, watching. A black man in shredded pants asked me for a handout. Beggars in New York! I felt I'd come to America too late. I felt cheated. I had Lillian's parting gift of one hundred dollars, of which I'd already spent twenty on food, and a bag of Florida oranges and grapefruit as a house present for Professorji.

This American beggar kept clawing at me, grabbing and touching in familiar ways, and when it became clear that I had nothing to give, he yelled, "You fucking bitch. Suck my fucking asshole, you fucking foreign bitch!" As passengers stared, he bounded up the down escalator.

In the taxi to Queens I wept hot, bewildered tears.

"Look, lady." In the rearview mirror I caught the driver's watchful glance. "You got American dollars?"

I nodded. He was from my part of the world, given to bitterness and suspicion. I could have spoken to him in Punjabi or Urdu, but I didn't. I wanted distance from all his greed and suspicions. "And if I run short," I said, "Professorji will take care of it. He was my husband's friend."

The driver said, "In Kabul I was a doctor. We have to be here living like dogs because they've taken everything from us."

I said nothing.

He went on about the wrongs. Bitterness seemed to buoy him, make him special. I would not immure myself as he had. Vijh & Wife was built on hope.

We took the bridge into Queens. On the streets I saw only more greed, more people like myself. New York was an archipelago of ghettos seething with aliens.

20

Y OU want to know what's wrong?" Darrel says on the phone. "Nothing's wrong. Everything's fine."

We're on a party line. The whole town seems to be hurting. I can hear the sighs of eavesdroppers. Last week a tenant farmer went to feed his hogs after supper. Three hours later his wife found him in the manure pit with a bullet in his head. His farm wasn't one of the ones in trouble, Bud said.

"I think you should go to Dalton. Go talk some more to those people about their golf-club idea."

"Dalton's not far enough," Darrel says. "I think I should go to Tahiti. Introduce beans and hogs to Tahiti, what do you think? I should get the hell out of Iowa."

"So, go to Tahiti."

"You're saying I'm running away from my problems."

"Running," I say. "Not running away." And to myself I say, *Why should you care what I think?*

The farm country is closing over Darrel. And over me, over Du. Tomorrow I'll plead with Bud.

I know what Darrel's going through.

I got out of Flushing within five months. Flushing was safe, a cocoon to hatch out of. Then one night—I was unrolling my sleeping mat on the floor of the Vadheras' living room—something came over me, and early the next morning I picked up my bag and my pocketbook and took the #7 train out of the ghetto. One more night and I would have died. Of what? I might have said then, of boredom, but boredom is only a manifestation of something worse.

Can *wanting* be fatal?

Professorji and his family put me up for five months— and it could have been five years, given the elasticity of the Indian family—just because I was the helpless widow of his favorite student. I was also efficient and uncomplaining, but they would have tolerated a clumsy whiner just as easily.

I want to be fair. Professorji is a generous man. Somehow, the trouble is in me. I had jumped a track. His kind of generosity wasn't good enough for me. It wasn't Prakash's, it wasn't Lillian Gordon's.

The family consisted of his aged parents and his recent bride, Nirmala, a girl of nineteen fresh from a village in the Patiala district. The marriage had been arranged about a year before. She was pretty enough to send a signal to any Indian in Flushing: *He may not look like much over here, but back in India this guy is considered quite a catch.*

In what I already considered "real life," meaning America, he was at least forty, thickening and having to color his hair. He had a new name in New York. Here he was "Dave," not Devinder, and not even Professor, though I never called him anything but Professorji. When he answered the phone, "Dave Vadhera here," even the Vadhera sounded English. It sounded like "David O'Hara."

They had no children. He had avoided marriage until he had saved enough to afford two children, and to educate them in New York. Male or female did not matter, he was a progressive man. They'd been trying, according to Nirmala, who blushingly confided the occasional marital intimacy. I took enough interest in their problem to look and listen for signs of dedicated activity. Perhaps they were more imaginative than I gave them credit for. Nirmala was nineteen: According to my forged passport, I was nineteen too, but I was a widow. She was in the game, I was permanently on the sidelines. Professorji blamed his long hours and back pains. She blamed impurities in the food.

Pleading lab work, Professorji was out of the house by seven o'clock, five days a week. They both came back at six

o'clock, harassed and foul-tempered, looking first for
snacks and tea, later for a major dinner.

Should anyone ask, I was her "cousin-sister."

Nirmala worked all day in a sari store on our block.
Selling upscale fabrics in Flushing indulged her taste for
glamour and sophistication. The shop also sold 220-volt
appliances, jewelry, and luggage. An adjacent shop under
the same Gujarati ownership sold sweets and spices, and
rented Hindi movies on cassettes. She was living in a little
corner of heaven.

Every night, Nirmala brought home a new Hindi film
for the VCR. Showings began promptly at nine o'clock,
just after an enormous dinner, and lasted till midnight.
They were Bombay's "B" efforts at best, commercial fail-
ures and quite a few famous flops, burnished again by the
dim light of nostalgia. I could not unroll my sleeping mat
until the film was over.

I felt my English was deserting me. During the parents'
afternoon naps, I sometimes watched a soap opera. The
American channels were otherwise never watched (Professorji's mother said, "There's so much English out there,
why do we have to have it in here?"), but for the Saturday-
morning Indian shows on cable. Nirmala brought plain
saris and salwar-kameez outfits for me from the shop so I
wouldn't have to embarrass myself or offend the old people

in cast-off American T-shirts. The sari patterns were for much older women, widows.

I could not admit that I had accustomed myself to American clothes. American clothes disguised my widowhood. In a T-shirt and cords, I was taken for a student. In this apartment of artificially maintained Indianness, I wanted to distance myself from everything Indian, everything Jyoti-like. To them, I was a widow who should show a proper modesty of appearance and attitude. If not, it appeared I was competing with Nirmala.

Flushing, with all its immigrant services at hand, frightened me. I, who had every reason to fear America, was intrigued by the city and the land beyond the rivers. The Vadheras, who would soon have saved enough to buy a small apartment building in Astoria, had retired behind ghetto walls.

To date in her year in America, Nirmala had exhausted the available stock of Hindi films on tape and was now renting Urdu films from a Pakistani store. She faced a grim future of unintelligible Bengali and Karnataka films. Everyone in Flushing seemed to know her craving. Visitors from India left tapes of popular Indian television series, and friends from Flushing were known to drive as far as New Jersey to check out the film holdings in the vast India emporia. They had a bookcase without books, stacked with television shows.

Professorji and Nirmala did not go out at night. "Why waste the money when we have everything here?" And truly they did. They had Indian-food stores in the block,

Punjabi newspapers and Hindi film magazines at the corner newsstand, and a movie every night without having to dress up for it. They had a grateful servant who took her pay in food and saris. The parents were long asleep, no need to indulge ritual pleasantries. In the morning, the same film had to be shown again to the parents. Then I walked the rewound cassette back to the rental store.

Professorji's parents, both in their eighties and rather adventurous for their age, demanded constant care. There were thirty-two Indian families in our building of fifty apartments, so specialized as to language, religion, caste, and profession that we did not need to fraternize with anyone but other educated Punjabi-speaking Hindu Jats. There were six families more or less like Professorji's (plus Punjabi-speaking Sikh families who seemed friendly in the elevator and politically tame, though we didn't mingle), and three of the families also had aged parents living in. Every morning, then, it was a matter of escorting the senior Vadheras to other apartments, or else serving tea and fried snacks to elderly visitors.

Sundays the Vadheras allowed themselves free time. We squeezed onto the sofa in the living room and watched videos of Sanjeev Kumar movies or of Amitabh. Or we went to visit with other Punjabi families in sparsely furnished, crowded apartments in the same building and watched their videos. Sundays were our days to eat too much and give in to nostalgia, to take the carom board out of the coat closet, to sit cross-legged on dhurries and matchmake marriages for adolescent cousins or younger siblings. Of course, as a widow, I did not participate. Remarriage was out of the question within the normal community. There were always much older widowers with children to look after who might consider me, and this, I know, was secretly discussed, but my married life and chance at motherhood were safely over.

Professorji's father always lost a little money at poker. Professorji always got a little drunk. When he got drunk he complained that America was killing him. "You want stress," he asked anyone who would listen, "or you want big bank balance?"

The old folks' complaints were familiar ones. In India the groom's mother was absolute tyrant of the household. The young bride would quiver under her commands. But in New York, with a working wife, the mother-in-law was denied her venomous authority. The bent old lady who required my arm to make her way from the television to the bathroom had been harboring hatred and resentment of *her* mother-in-law for sixty-five years. Now that she *finally* had the occasion to vent it, Nirmala wasn't around to receive it. This was the tenor of all the old people's complaints—we have followed our children to America, and look what happens to us! Our sons are selfish. Our daughters want to work and stay thin. All the time, this rush-rush. What to do? There are no grandchildren for us to play with. This country has drained my son of his dum. This country has turned my daughter-in-law into a barren field. If we are doomed to die here, at least let us enjoy the good things of America: friends from our village, plentiful food, VCRs, air conditioning.

I felt myself deteriorating. I had gained so much weight I couldn't get into the cords even when I tried. I couldn't understand the soap operas. I didn't know the answers to game shows. And so I cooked, shopped, and cleaned, tended the old folks, and made conversation with Professorji when he got home.

Professorji was a good man, by his lights, but he didn't seem the same caring teacher who, in sleek blue American aerograms only months before, had tempted Prakash, his best engineering student, to leave the petty, luckless world of Jullundhar. Flushing was a neighborhood in Jullundhar. I was spiraling into depression behind the fortress of Punjabiness. Some afternoons when Professorji was out working, and Nirmala was in her shop, and the old Vadheras were snoring through their siestas, I would find myself in the bathroom with the light off, head down on the cold, cracked rim of the sink, sobbing from unnamed, unfulfilled wants. In Flushing I felt immured. An imaginary brick wall topped with barbed wire cut me off from the past and kept me from breaking into the future. I was a prisoner doing unreal time. Without a green card, even a forged one (I knew at least four men in our building who had bought themselves resident alien cards for between two and three thousand dollars), I didn't feel safe going outdoors. If I had a green card, a job, a goal, *happiness* would appear out of the blue.

One Monday—after a particularly boisterous Sunday— Professorji came home around two in the afternoon and caught me crying as he barged into the dark bathroom. He seemed helpless before my grief. I tried to stop my sobbing and swallowing, but the more I tried, the harder the tears came.

Professorji turned on the light, and with it the noisy, hateful fan. "You're like a daughter to me," he said, in his stiff, shy way. "Has anybody been treating you like a servant?"

Disappointments tumbled out of me. I told him I wanted a green card more than anything else in the world, that a green card was freedom.

Professorji put the toilet lid down and sat on it cautiously. He lit a cigarette and held it pinched between thumb and index finger, as my brothers used to. "A green card," he said, "is an expensive but not an impossible proposition. For the rich, such a matter is arranged daily."

"Then arrange it!" I begged. "Please! I'm dying in this limbo." I'd sign any IOU he wanted, at any interest rate he fixed, if he would advance the two or three thousand.

"You?" Professorji smiled. "You think you have enough skills to pay me back so much money within my lifetime?" He suggested I send word to my brothers to see if they could pay him in rupees. "For Prakash's sake," he said, "I'll make this concession. I'll take rupees." He quoted black-market exchange rates that weren't outrageously unfair.

I calculated in my head. Three thousand dollars would come to fifty thousand rupees. My brothers were generous, loyal, ingenious men, but they couldn't get together fifty thousand fixing motor scooters in Hasnapur. I wouldn't demand it of them. Still, Professorji didn't have to know that.

I glared down at the embarrassed and unhappy man sitting on the toilet lid. "The card is for me, and I shall make the payments." I had to believe that given a chance I could make the payments.

"And how do you think you'll do that?" he said. He stood up and flushed his cigarette. Then he said, "All right. I shall make all the necessary arrangements. But this is not something we want to discuss with my wife and parents."

I was so thrown by his quick turnaround that I dropped to my knees and touched his feet to thank him, as I would have done in Hasnapur. He walked slowly out into the hall, as though my desperation hadn't gone head to head with his generosity in the tiny bathroom.

Professorji came through, but he was emotionally tight, with Nirmala, with his parents, with me. I was grateful, and I admired him, but I didn't understand him. He was secretive, he was parsimonious with his affections. I remembered Prakash's rage against Jagtiani, his depressions, his glee. He told me everything, took pleasure in my adventures, small as they were. Nirmala had no idea where her husband worked—he never told her. "What if there's an accident?" I asked, and she smiled, like a child. "*He* will know," she said, using the pronoun. She had no idea what he did. He was following an ancient prescription for marital accord: silence, order, authority. So was she: submission, beauty, innocence.

One day his father cut his head open on the bathtub faucet. I couldn't decide, because I didn't know enough about the old man's immigration status and medical insurance, if I should rush him by taxi to a hospital or call the emergency squad. Old Mrs. Vadhera was screaming for a doctor, a priest, and her son. I called Queens College and asked for Professor Vadhera. They asked which department, and I didn't know. They checked every variant spelling, every department, and couldn't find him. Try Queensborough College, the woman suggested. Or LaGuardia Community. I did. Nothing.

Leaving the old woman in charge, I hurried down to Nirmala's sari shop. She was sitting in the back with a Coke, watching an Urdu film. Scurrying through old papers, she found an address for *him*. The Almighty Him. It was a street number, not a college.

Flushing was not the downtown of dreams I'd conjured from the aerogram back in Jullundhar. And Professorji was not a professor. He was an importer and sorter of human hair. The hair came in great bundles from middlemen in villages as small as Hasnapur all over India. The middlemen shipped the hair in switches. Every weekday Professorji sat from eight o'clock till six on a kitchen ladder-stool in a room he rented in the basement of the Khyber Bar BQ measuring and labeling the length and thickness of each separate hair.

Junk hair he sold to wigmakers. Fine hair to instrument makers. Eventually, scientific instruments and the U.S. Defense Department. It was no exaggeration to say that the security of the free world, in some small way, depended on the hair of Indian village women. His integrity as a man of science, and as a businessman, rested on the absolute guarantee that hair from Dave Vadhera met the highest standards and had been personally selected.

As for his father, he said he'd call a doctor friend, an uncertified but still hopeful Delhi doctor working as a technician for a blood bank, who lived three floors down, to come around and bandage the wound. He acted more upset that I'd found him; *found him out*. He suspected that I'd deliberately shamed him, using the excuse of an injured father to pry information out of Nirmala. Now she'd get suspicious if *I* didn't talk about the university and his labs and all his assistants.

I told him not to worry. I would.

Actually, he said, he still was a scientist. America hadn't robbed him of his self-respect. "No synthetic material has the human hair's tensile strength. How to gauge humidity without strands?" He picked out a long black hair from the 24-inch tray. "Like this beautiful one. How to read the weather?"

A hair from some peasant's head in Hasnapur could travel across oceans and save an American meteorologist's reputation. Nothing was rooted anymore. Everything was in motion.

"You could sell your hair, if you wanted to. It is eighteen

inches at least, I think. We are purchasing Indian ladies' hair only. Indian women are purists, they're cleansing their hair with berries or yogurt only, they're not ruining their hair with shampoos, gels, dyes, and permanents. American women have horrible hair—this I have learned since settling here. Their hair lacks virginity and innocence."

I got the point. He needed to work here, but he didn't have to like it. He had sealed his heart when he'd left home. His real life was in an unlivable land across oceans. He was a ghost, hanging on.

That's when he offered to introduce me to the master forger, another renter in the Khyber basement. He made up a fake bill of sale, my future hair when it was twenty-four inches, for three thousand dollars. He was buying my silence for his shame, and I felt the shame as well.

A week later, I found myself calling Kate Gordon-Feldstein.

21

A<small>LL</small> Saturday Du shuts himself in his room, reshuffling circuits, combining new functions. Why should a radio produce only sound, a light switch only light? Du's light automatically brings music, since for him the two are intimately connected. All his lights are on dimmers, the dimmers scan the FM band as they control the lights. Efficiency, he would say—why should dimmers confine themselves to one, boring function? He can disconnect as well. Why should a bathroom fan be attached to the light, forcing people to shit in the dark if they don't like the noise, or don't mind the smell?

Like Prakash, he has a surgeon's touch. He transforms the crude appliances that he touches. Months after he arrived, while Bud was still in the hospital, he rigged my alarm clock to the coffee maker in the kitchen. He transformed remote-control garage-door openers into door openers for a chair-bound man. He's attached his Walkman to the car's stereo, giving it a tape deck. His favorite phrase is "Zap it." He is the son Prakash and I might have had.

Bud is gratified, but not that impressed. He says it's because Du never worked it out as a child. Technology's a giant birthday cake for him. He never slaved over model trains, never built model planes. Bud notices a lot of Du's genius is for scavenging, adaptation, appropriate technology.

The brightest boy in the camps. The boy who survived.

"Still at it?" I look in on him because I am lonely. We are by ourselves in the house this weekend. Bud's in Des Moines for another conference. The themes sound pretty much the same to me; this time it's "Transitional Agriculture: Impact on Farmers and Bankers." Bud's been in demand since the shooting. All in all, he jokes, even cheap celebrity is not worth the price. Something's gotten out of hand in the heartland, says the Elsa County Mental Health Center consultant who's coordinated this weekend's conference. He'd hate to use an old-fashioned word like "civility," but that seems to be fitting. The drought's a catalyst, it's not the problem.

Last week in Dalton County a farmer dug a trench all

around his banker's house with stolen backhoe equipment. On TV he said, "Call it a moat of hate."

Over by Osage a man beat his wife with a spade, then hanged himself in his machine shed.

I've started to keep the front door locked when Bud's away. I want my family under one roof, the door bolted against nameable dreads.

"Right, still at it," says Du.

"How's it going?"

"Okay. Everything's okay."

"Do you want to invite Scott over?"

"No, Mom. Scott's good for watching TV with. I'm a gearhead, remember?"

"Where do you learn all this engineering, Du?"

"It's not engineering. It's recombinant electronics. I have altered the gene pool of the common American appliance. I have spliced the gene of a Black & Decker paint sprayer onto the gear drive of a repaired Mixmaster. I have created a multi-use super air blower with a variable-speed main-drive. I leave the application to the Scotts of the world. And another thing—I didn't have to *learn* it, it's what I do. Like Dad handles money and you—" He fumbled his needle-nosed pliers. "Shit!"

"And I what?"

"Handle Dad."

I take a step inside. "Well, he has special needs, doesn't he?" I watch him part a mass of wires with his pliers, then reach for his soldering gun. "I can do that, you know. I've had experience. Small, skinny fingers and all. I've handled a soldering gun."

156

"Congratulations."

"I understand circuitry." I pick up the soldering gun, and he pinches the wires together over the terminal as I drop a bright bead of smoking silver on it.

"I've also killed a man, you know. There's nothing in this world that's too terrible."

I drop a second bead on the next connection.

"I know," he says. "So have I. More than one."

I go back downstairs and wait for Bud to call me from his hotel. He'll call at 11:05, after the rates change. He has his routines and his frugalities. He is the most reliable, considerate man I know.

At 11:05 the phone rings. I cradle it. I let it ring against my chest. Upstairs Du is gutting another scavenged tuner. He has plans, he says. My suggestion was to fill it with soil and plant some corn or beans inside. Keep the knobs and dials on the outside. From the streets of Saigon to Iowa State engineering school.

"Maybe I'll make a bomb," he said, and cackled like a mad scientist.

"Sweetheart," Bud says. I try to picture him in a hotel room. Orrin Lacey, the Ag Loans man who drove Bud to the conference, will have helped Bud change into pajamas and settle in the center of the hotel bed, then gone down to the bar. Bud's teeth are flossed raw and smell slightly of spearmint. His feet are warmly socked. He has started to wear socks to bed because his circulation has slowed since the accident. "I hope you've had a better day."

"That bad?" I say.

"Worse. I had a guy come up to me after my paper. The guy said, 'When I shoot, I don't shoot just to maim.' Then he taped a pamphlet to my chair. *Jews Take Over Our Farmland.* Orrin tore it off."

"Be careful out there," I say.

"Des Moines's the pits. It used to be a pretty little city. I could be proud of Des Moines wherever I traveled."

"Be proud of Elsa County," I said. "Be proud of Baden. You practically built it."

I think he must be crying in his hotel room. Crying comes over him suddenly these days. They call it post-traumatic syndrome. Small things, mildly depressing things, suddenly become too poignant to bear.

"There's so many pretty places I want to show you and I can't. Things weren't always this ugly, Jane."

22

WHEN I met Kate Gordon-Feldstein in her loft, she said, "They'll love you. Really. You don't have to be scared of them."

I was just an hour out of Flushing. Professorji didn't have this number.

Her corner loft was *huge*, an entire floor in the garment district. It could have held five of the Flushing apartments. Two walls were solid windows, looking out on somber buildings and a patch of sky. It had been a dance space, then a television studio. A third wall had been converted into a series of darkrooms with appropriate drainage. The remaining wall was gypsum board painted in strips of very bright colors: parrot green, blueberry yogurt, crushed raspberry, even glossy black, where hundreds of photos were pinned. Clotheslines crisscrossed from wall to wall, post to post, all of them clipped and pinned with drying prints.

As we talked, she was taking pictures of me from every angle. "What a great face," she said.

They had no real furniture, just a baby grand piano and three futons, two folded over as sofas and the third left as their unmade bed. Filing cabinets spewed clothes. Her husband was out of town, on a shoot. The incidental clutter was astounding to me, after the order of Professorji's apartment: chair frames without seats, wet towels on the floor, magazines and newspapers stuffed into a wicker clothes hamper, cardboard containers from a takeout place on the window ledge.

It thrilled me. Sunlight smeared one wall of windows. It spoke to me of possibility, that one could live like this and not be struck down.

I remembered Kate's book of photographs of migrant workers that Lillian, the proud mother, had shown off to me back in Fowlers Key. That book had brought back such sharp memories of Hasnapur that I'd cried. It was now only a few months later, but I didn't think I could cry over Hasnapur, ever again.

I took it now to mean this was what a girl from a swampy backwater could accomplish. I had wandered into that same clearing. I had seen those same women and children, or ones just like them. And then I had seen them again, but really for the first time, thanks to Kate, in a prize-winning book. This loft, if it stood for anything beyond incredible good luck in the Manhattan housing market, was also a reflection of her mother's taste, put into practice by a dutiful daughter: simple, ample, plain, functional, frugal, even spiritual.

Kate said, "I know what you're thinking. If they're friends of mine, they must be just as messy. Don't worry, you won't have to pick up after them. You'll be looking after Duff. The Hayeses are terminally neat."

"Duff is a girl's name?"

I had just escaped from the tidiness, the neatness, of my benefactors in Flushing. I'd just abandoned whatever chance at security I had in the world. I tried to put it all in words while Kate circled me, snapping away from the floor, from the chair frames, from the window ledge. I didn't have that much English, but what little bit I had came tumbling out, frustrated by all the months in Flushing. I had come to America and lost my English.

"Oh, you did the right thing," said Kate. "Don't apologize for what you did, it's heroic."

My note to Professorji had been properly self-condemning. My unhappiness was all my fault. Their generosity was more than I, poor wretch, deserved. Hold the memory of Prakash as dear as I do. I promised to pay back any debts I might have incurred (this deliberately fuzzy in case Nirmala read it). I thanked them all for the lessons they had taught me.

I had meant the note sincerely; they had taught me a

great deal about surviving as an Indian in New York. If I had been a different person with a different set of experiences—if I had been another Nirmala, as they'd expected—then Professorji's lesson would be life-affirming, invaluable, inexpressibly touching. They had kept a certain kind of Punjab alive, even if that Punjab no longer existed. They let nothing go, lest everything be lost.

Kate, the ironist, heard only contempt, and began to laugh. "You have a wicked sense of humor, Jasmine, and so do the Hayeses," she said. "You'll love them. They'll love you."

Behind a dry-wall partition I heard some rattling and scratching. "Oh, that's Sam," Kate said. "He hates being shut in. He knows there's company, and he positively adores Duff. Do you mind animals? I don't think the Hayeses have any livestock. Duff's allergic to cat dander, I know that for a fact. That's what's so nice about Sam. No dander."

I lied. "I'm not afraid of animals."

"Well, if you're sure you don't mind, I'll let Sam out."

She carried him to the center of the room. Only the wrinkled, crested, wattled green head peered out from under the crook of her arm. The tail drooped well below her knees.

Sam was an animal I couldn't name. A small dinosaur? A giant lizard? She let him down. He stared and stretched, turning his head in every direction, yawning and hissing, his long black tongue flicking like a whip. Then he bounded across the wooden floor to sniff me out, then to paw my leg and begin to climb. Kate took out her camera again. "Oh, your face, Jasmine—priceless!"

I picked him up and held him. Truly, I had been reborn. Indian village girls do not hold large reptiles on their laps. They would scream at the swipe of a dry tongue, the basilisk stare of a beady eye. The relationship of an Indian, any Indian, to a reptile, any reptile, is that of a fisherman to a fish.

A giant, hideous version of a gecko lay snorting and hissing and tongue-flicking on my lap. The boys in my village used to climb into the corners of our rooms, catch the house lizards, then hang them by the neck from branches of the lichee trees. We'd watch them twitch and turn until the crows discovered them. Then we'd sit around and watch the birds pull them apart, like worms after a rainstorm.

"Sam's a marine iguana. Jerry was on a shoot in the Galápagos and poor old Sam hatched right at his feet. Sam's on the cover of *Smithsonian*, in fact. He thinks he's a dog and he's ashamed of being vegetarian. We thought he'd be death on roaches. Instead, we have to purée lettuce."

Sam hissed. He seemed to like a scratching on his belly. He flipped right over. I had never seen anything so ugly.

"Big baby," said Kate.

I looked into his beady little eyes, his ugly wattled face. Sam, I thought, we're both a long way from home, aren't we? What'll we do? Look after little girls? There's no going back, is there?

He started thumping his tail against my shins, hard and painfully. Kate called it his kick of contentment, he was happy with me.

23

I BECAME an American in an apartment on Claremont Avenue across the street from a Barnard College dormitory. I lived with Taylor and Wylie Hayes for nearly two years. Duff was my child; Taylor and Wylie were my parents, my teachers, my family.

I entered their life on a perfect spring Sunday. Kate and I left Sam in his corner of the loft, baking on a rock pile underneath a sunlamp, in the middle of a child's plastic wading pool, and took a bus all the way up Broadway to 116th Street, at the gates of Columbia University. The sky had a special penetrating blueness, the temperature and humidity made it seem we were breathing through our skin. We went down the hill toward the river, then turned in at the first building. The street was Claremont Avenue and all the apartments belonged to Columbia teachers, true professorjis. I expected the air itself to crackle with so much intelligence.

Wylie and Taylor and their little girl, Duff, met us with tea and biscuits. They were in their early thirties, and dressed like students in T-shirts and cords. Taylor had teeth as crooked as mine—the first crooked teeth I'd seen in America—with a gap between his front teeth wide enough to hold a matchstick. He had a blondish beard. Wylie was tall and blond, thin as a schoolgirl, with a pair of dark glasses pushed high in her hair, and a pair of regular glasses resting on her chest, held by a chain around her neck. Duff immediately asked my name and where I was from. "You know where India is, darling. Remember, we found it on the map." She took out a piece of paper and tried to spell my name. I had never seen a small child, especially a girl, who could immediately relate to adults, call them by their first names, and break into their conversations.

She asked Kate, "Where's my Sammy?" Kate reminded her that Sam and city buses were not on good terms. The one time she'd taken him on a bus, wrapped like a baby but for his breathing holes, the crested tail had popped from the blanket, the tongue had darted, and a man sitting next to them had drawn a knife in self-defense. Thereafter she left him at home in what Duff called Sammy's Ocean.

I asked what kind of pets the Hayeses had. Fortunately, the university permitted nothing as exotic as iguanas and snakes, only the usual dogs, cats, rabbits, hamsters, gerbils—none of which Duff could tolerate because of allergies.

"We might have to move if Duff wants an ostrich or something," said Taylor. Duff giggled. Kate prompted me to smile.

Silence fell. I nibbled a biscuit.

"I hope $95 a week is satisfactory," said Wylie. "I've checked around, and that's a little low, but there really shouldn't be any other expenses—"

I had not imagined money, *dollars*, for sleeping with a child. "That is very good," I said.

"I'm not going to ask you for references, Jasmine," she went on. "Kate's already told us something about you. Lillian Gordon's word is solid gold with us. You will be part of the family. Families don't go around requiring references."

"Anyway, Sam already approved you," said Taylor. "Being cold-blooded, he doesn't warm to many people. In fact, he has a godlike perspective on the whole mammal class."

He smiled his crooked-toothed smile, and I began to fall in love. I mean, I fell in love with what he represented to me, a professor who served biscuits to a servant, smiled at her, and admitted her to the broad democracy of his joking, even when she didn't understand it. It seemed entirely American. I was curious about his life, not repulsed. I wanted to know the way such a man lives in this country. I wanted to watch, be a part of it. He seemed wondrously extravagant, that Sunday morning.

"He likes to be rubbed on the stomach," I said.

"Fastest way to an iguana's heart. Everyone knows *that*."

"Oh, Daddy, *really*." Duff frowned.

"I can tell you are a refined person," Wylie continued. "We ask only for affection and intelligence in dealing with Duff. A child raised by affectionate, intelligent people with a good sense of humor will grow up all right."

"That, and getting into Brearley," Taylor remarked.

"I don't think I have much humor," I said. The decent Americans I'd seen on television seemed a whimsical people, always making jokes, like Kate and Taylor. Wylie was a serious woman, all duty and business, like Lillian Gordon. The ones I'd met in person were not too funny. Humor's the hardest thing to translate.

Duff, she said, was enrolled in a play school at the Riverside Church. This would leave my mornings free. There would be lunch to prepare, her nap, and maybe strolls in the park or trips around town. Very little television. I was to stimulate her with questions, engage her with stories, read to her, go to museums, puppet shows, galleries. Next year she might be in an all-day school, which would leave me free to investigate classes myself. They'd help any way they could.

"You're probably tired of Americans assuming that if you're from India or China or the Caribbean you must be good with children," said Wylie.

"Thank you," I replied. What else could I say? I had never heard such a thing. The Chinese I had always thought of as genetically cruel to women and children— even in Hasnapur we knew about foot-binders—and my experience of Caribbeans was a mixture of fear and pity.

"Ancient American custom, dark-skinned mammies. Don't be flattered by it," said Taylor.

"In fact," said Wylie, "we assume there'll be times when you absolutely hate her and want to wring her neck."

"We suggest counting to ten first," said Taylor.

Duff was drawing and coloring and didn't raise her head.

Wylie showed me around. "Sixteen hundred square feet," she said, "so I don't think either of us will feel crowded." She opened and shut doors of closets, pulled open drawers on the smoothest of rollers, revealing gadgets I had no idea how to use, patted dials on the dishwasher, and rested fingertips on the start-up panel of a sleek microwave. "If you have a thing about radiation, you don't have to use it," she said. "You just let us know when we upset you, all right?"

"I don't have a thing about radiation," I said.

We stood on the narrow balcony and looked out on Claremont Avenue as Wylie gave me facts about Taylor, Duff, and herself. Taylor, a professorji, was an expert in an area of subnuclear particle physics. Wylie was a book editor for a publisher on Park Avenue. About her work she said, dismissively, "You can call my writers the New Sob Sisters. We ghoul around courtrooms and develop projects." She explained about the money to be made signing up celebrity interviews, writing about divorces and drug cases, society murders, child abuse, and rape. She made them sound like grave robbers.

I didn't have the slightest understanding of anything they said, and they didn't bother explaining. I liked that, the assumption behind it.

Wylie said that Duff was adopted.

"Low sperm count," she explained.

I blushed, but neither Wylie nor Taylor noticed.

"Hockey injury," Taylor protested.

They planned to tell Duff everything when she was old enough. They'd even let her meet her natural mother, currently a sophomore at Iowa State University. Their lawyer had placed ads in small-town Iowa and Nebraska and Kansas newspapers, asking pregnant unwed girls to contact him. Wylie and Taylor were paying for the girl's education. I remember thinking an Iowa newspaper must be in a language called Iowan, like a Punjabi or a Spanish newspaper. I liked the mystery. Duff looked perfectly American.

"We could have gotten a child out of Paraguay," Taylor explained. "The Needhams on the sixth floor got their baby from Paraguay. They had to go down and hang around for six weeks in this nothing village full of Nazi war criminals, and the way they described the whole thing, it sounded awful, sort of like a direct sale."

I could not imagine a non-genetic child. A child that was not my own, or my husband's, struck me as a monstrous idea. Adoption was as foreign to me as the idea of widow remarriage.

I looked out into the dorm windows across Claremont Avenue. The windows were long, bright, shadeless rectangles of light. No window shades, no secrets. Barnard women were studying cross-legged on narrow beds, changing T-shirts, clowning with Walkmans clamped to their heads. They wore nothing under their shirts and sweaters. Men were in their room. Even on the first morning I saw naked bodies combing their hair in front of dresser mirrors. Truly there was no concept of shame in this society. I'd die before a Sob Sister asked me about Half-Face.

The love I felt for Taylor that first day had nothing to do with sex. I fell in love with his world, its ease, its careless confidence and graceful self-absorption. I wanted to become the person they thought they saw: humorous, intelligent, refined, affectionate. Not illegal, not murderer, not widowed, raped, destitute, fearful. In Flushing, I had lived defensively in the midst of documented rectitude. I did not want to live legally if it also meant living like a refugee.

"We'll give you Taylor's study," Wylie said. "We'll move his junk into the dining room. You'll have your own room that way."

"Junk!" Taylor laughed. "Junk!" The gap made him look sardonic. Back in his hockey-crazy town in upstate New York, he'd lost a number of teeth and they were never replaced with bridgework, so the teeth he had left—chipped teeth, crooked teeth—had drifted and settled deep in his gums, leaving gaps between them. The teeth seemed to mock whatever he said. "For you, Jasmine, I'll be homeless. For you, Japanese research will widen the meson gap. We'll have your room ready by next Sunday."

"Then where will Duff sleep?"

"Her room, of course."

"Not with me?" I could not imagine a small child sleeping alone. I had trouble enough with it myself, never having spent a night alone until I got to Lillian Gordon's. That was Lillian's pride: that she could give me Kate's old room, by myself, not with the Kanjobal women. I would have preferred sleeping on a floor mat. In Flushing I could at least hear the snoring of Professorji and his father. I had lain awake in the Florida cottage, watching ghosts flit across the ceiling, wrap themselves in the curtains, creak from room to room. When Kate had told me of a possible job looking after a child, I had imagined myself in a narrow bed with a baby, and the thought had brought me comfort.

"Who will I sleep with?" I asked.

"What you do on your own time is your business," said Wylie. "But show discretion, for Duff's sake. I hope you understand."

"Let us check him out first, is what she means," said Taylor.

"Who?" I asked.

Kate came over. "Can we start again?" she suggested.

On Sunday Taylor's computer station was still by the window in the study, his racing bike hanging like art on the wall, and his windjamming equipment in the closet. "Give me a couple more days," he said. "There's another breakthrough in the lab." He was out early, back late. I prayed he was not sorting hair. Wylie put on a martyr's face. I'd been sleeping on a cot in his room, folding it up by day. All my T-shirts and cords fitted into a plastic bag in the closet.

They thought I wanted a room of my own. I had no way of telling them it wasn't necessary, that I worried about Duff all alone with her animal paintings and stuffed dolls. She was a lovely child, easy to look after. She was the only American, at the time, that I was capable of totally under-standing. For her, I was a wise adult without an accent. For me, she was an American friend whose language I under-stood and humor I could laugh at. And she laughed at mine. I did have a sense of humor.

She was a pale child with pale eyes and pale hair. When she raced ahead of me in Riverside Park and I pretended to chase her, it was like chasing a milkweed parachute or a feather. I was learning about the stores, the neighborhood, shopping, from her.

Sleeping in Duff's room was supposed to be temporary, but she and I quickly fixed that. We moved my cot in. I prayed I'd be allowed to stay. I planted the idea with her. To Wylie I said, "I don't mind, really," and copied her look of a put-upon saint.

*　*　*

If Duff had been born in Kansas, I think now, that's where I would have headed when I was fleeing New York. Who lays out the roadways of our futures? What if! What if the Hayeses' lawyer had taken out ads in Nebraska? In Wisconsin?

The apartment was stocked like a museum. Wylie and Taylor weren't simple acquisitors. Unlike the Vadheras, they bought useless things, silly things, ugly things— wooden ducks, two wooden Indians, a wood cutout of Carmen Miranda—and arranged them in clusters. Some of them seemed offensive to blacks or women or Red Indians. There were slave-auction posters from New Orleans in 1850, speaking of healthy wenches and strong bucks; old color prints celebrating the massacre of an entire Indian village down to the last baby; a poster of a naked woman with parts of her body labeled choice, prime, or chuck, as in a butcher shop.

In the bathroom they hung mounted prints of flowers: *Dauphinelle elevée, Pimprenelle cultivée, Hélianthe commun.* I had memorized the names and spellings before learning the words were French and they didn't grow here. I took in everything. Every morning, the news sank into my brain, and stayed. Language on the street, on the forbidden television, at the Hayeses' dinners, where I sat like a guest and only helped with the serving (and, increasingly, controlled the menu), all became *my* language, which I learned like a child, from the first words up. The squatting fields of Hasnapur receded fast.

My first live-in day on Claremont, Wylie showed me the powder room in the hall. "That's more or less exclusively for you and Duff," she said, "but the shower you'll have to share with us." For a second I caught a hesitation, an opacity, in her wide brown eyes, and then the eyes brightened again. She was apologizing for having just one shower, but I'd misinterpreted. I'd even panicked, wondering where the servants' shower was, if I was to share it with the doorman and janitor in the basement. I never showered when they were in. American showers still delighted me, despite the inevitable, daily association with Flamingo Court, with preparation for death, with the knowledge that a naked body was outside the door, waiting to rape again, perhaps to kill. Touching a tap and having the water hot-hot, and plentiful, was still a sensual thrill.

When Wylie talked of me on the phone, she called me her "caregiver." "I don't know what I'd do without her. Jasmine's a real find. Not like that last one who threw the front-door keys in the incinerator when she walked out on us." Or: "I won't say I'll definitely be at the fund-raiser until I've checked Tuesday night out with my caregiver." Caregiver. The word sang off my tongue. I was a professional, like a schoolteacher or a nurse. I wasn't a maidservant.

In Hasnapur the Mazbi woman who'd stoked our hearth or spread our flaking, dried-out adobe walls with watered cow dung had been a maidservant. Wylie made me feel her younger sister. I was family, and I was professional.

*   *   *

Taylor called me "Jase" as he stumbled around the kitchen in his wrinkled kimono and ate Grape Nuts cereal standing at the counter. I can still see him smiling his goofy smile at Duff and me, and managing to spoon some of the cereal into his beard. At the time I told myself that it was his goofiness and his clowning that I loved. He was the only man I knew who didn't mind getting caught looking silly. Prakash'd wanted to be infallible, and Professorji'd acted pompous. Taylor was fun. Could I really have not guessed that I was head over heels in love with Taylor? I liked everything he said or did. I liked the name he gave me: Jase. Jase was a woman who bought herself spangled heels and silk chartreuse pants. On my day off I took my week's salary (every Saturday night Wylie put the $95 in cash in an envelope with a Happy Face and a "Thanks!" Magic Markered on it and propped it against the Cuisinart) and blew too much of it in stores along Broadway and even in the big department stores.

I should have saved; a cash stash is the only safety net. I'd learned that if nothing else from the scrimping Vadheras. Jyoti would have saved. But Jyoti was now a *sati*-goddess; she had burned herself in a trash-can–funeral pyre behind a boarded-up motel in Florida. Jasmine lived for the future, for Vijh & Wife. Jase went to movies and lived for today. In my closet hung satin blouses with vampish necklines, in my dresser lingerie I was too shy to wear in a room I shared with Duff. Profligate squandering was my way of breaking with the panicky, parsimonious ghettos of Flushing.

For every Jasmine the reliable caregiver, there is a Jase the prowling adventurer. I thrilled to the tug of opposing forces. I prayed my job as Duff's "day mummy" would last forever.

Day mummy: this is how the name came about. One weekday morning in my first month, Wylie came out into the hall ready for work in the little black skirt and the biggish checkered jacket with the mannish padded shoulders she felt good in, and heard Duff beg me, "Mummy, can you finish that story about Nachos and Yama when we go to the park?" Duff had climbed into my lap and locked her fists around my neck in a wet hug.

"Nachiketas," I corrected, "not Nachos."

In the hall I heard Wylie's briefcase close with a pained click. All the stories I told Duff were about gods and demons and mortals.

Duff took my face in her hands and begged again, "Mummy, can we go to the park right now and feed bread to the birds?"

Wylie said, without looking at me, "I have to leave for work now. But we need to talk. After dinner let's talk. Taylor'll be here, too."

I said, "Duff thinks of me as her day mummy. Day mummy takes her to the Y, to the park, to the market. You're her mom. Why do we need to talk after dinner? Talk makes trouble, it doesn't solve it."

"I should know how to handle this, but I don't," Wylie said as she went out the door. "The main thing is not to confuse a child. See you tonight."

But I didn't see her that night. She called Taylor at seven

to say that one of her Sob Sisters was about to be sued for having defamed her subject's character ("The creep beat his wife to death with a metal bar, for god's sake") and that she was having to meet with a lawyer. I put Duff to bed, which was something Wylie liked to do herself, and Taylor read Duff and me a paper he was writing on weak gravity, in a room that was dark except for the yellow glow of a table lamp and the purple glow of the fish tank. He made it funny, choosing neighborhood and household examples for anything technical. "Weak gravity is what keeps your dreams inside your head so they don't go flying out," he said. "It's what keeps Jase and Duff together," he said, smiling sweetly, "so they don't fly off the bed at night. When you look around, weak gravity is everywhere."

We didn't have our talk. We didn't have to. Fish rippled their phosphorescent stripes inside the tank. The water gurgled, always clean, always warm.

The next morning I put my arms around Wylie. She cried. She said, We're family; in a family don't sisters sometimes fight? Duff cried, too. Then she said, "Mummy go to work now. Day mummy light her sticks and drive out ghosts."

There were other day mummies in the building. We were a sorority that met in the laundry room and in the park. Two of them I got to know quite well, Letitia from Trinidad, and Jamaica from Barbados. Letitia was a grumbler and Jamaica was a snob. Lettie would say of her boss, the interior decorator who'd traveled all the way to Paraguay to adopt a baby, "What she t'ink? Slavery makin a big comeback? Jassie girl, minute my sponsorship come t'rough, we gotta unionize." Jamaica said in her haughty Britishy voice, "Do I look like someone who guzzles vodka or steals pork chops? Do I look like a common person?" Every night, Jamaica claimed, she cried her heart out. I imagined a polyester-filled pillow squelchy with monsoonsful of tears. She'd been promised a groom. She'd come to Brooklyn with the best of intentions, and then the low-life scum had deserted her. She was too proud to return. She wasn't born to be a maid, that was her refrain. Her mummy and daddy'd die if they found out she was cleaning up dirt, especially white folks' dirt, in America.

I felt lucky. My pillow was dry, a launch pad for lift-off. Taylor, Wylie, and Duff were family. America may be fluid and built on flimsy, invisible lines of weak gravity, but I was a dense object, I had landed and was getting rooted. I had controlled my spending and now sat on an account that was rapidly growing. Every day I was being paid for something new. I'd thought Professorji out in Flushing was exceptional, back when I didn't have a subway token. Now I saw how easy it was. Since I was spending nothing on food and rent, the money was piling up.

*   *   *

In the second year, with Duff in school full days, Taylor arranged a part-time job for me at Columbia in the Mathematics Department, answering phones. I worked six hours a day, at six dollars an hour, suddenly doubling my caregiver salary. I offered to move out, which seemed the American thing to do, but Wylie begged me to stay.

With Columbia employment I was eligible for free tuition in Columbia extension courses, if I could convince them to overlook the fact that I was a sixth-grade dropout. There was nurse's training at Columbia-Presbyterian. There was English as a Second Language, but they told me my English was too good. When I flipped through the General Studies catalogue, I saw a thousand courses I wanted to take, in science, in art, in languages. There was nothing that seemed too exotic, nothing that did not seem essential to my future.

The Indian Languages Department used me as a Punjabi reader ("Perfect Jullundhari!" The instructor beamed. He was making a linguistic atlas of the Punjab); they asked if I wanted to teach a beginning section someday, or tutor some graduate students. I chose the tutoring. A man with a Ford Foundation grant to study land reform in the Punjab came to me. Executives being sent to Delhi came to me. They asked if forty dollars an hour was too insulting, given Berlitz rates, and I said no, not for a good cause. One executive brought me flowers and wine, another took me out to dinner and asked me if I was . . . otherwise engaged. I paid back Professorji in a single check.

*   *   *

In America, nothing lasts. I can say that now and it doesn't shock me, but I think it was the hardest lesson of all for me to learn. We arrive so eager to learn, to adjust, to participate, only to find the monuments are plastic, agreements are annulled. Nothing is forever, nothing is so terrible, or so wonderful, that it won't disintegrate.

In the early summer of my second year, Wylie fell out of love with Taylor and into love with an economist named Stuart Eschelman who lived two buildings up the street. She told me her problem before she told Taylor. "It's all so messy. Taylor's such a sweetheart, and there's Duff and Stuart's three kids, but this is my chance at real happiness. What can I do? I've got to go for it, right?"

They had met caroling on Claremont before Christmas, and love had taken its slow, sweet course. The economist's wife was a professor at NYU, but on leave to the World Bank, somewhere in West Africa. Wylie showed me Stuart's book, on the measurement of poverty. I looked through the charts and figures. Poverty had shape, clarity, its own crystalline beauty.

"He's wonderful, Jase," said Wylie. "It's the real thing this time."

She stuck a mug of black coffee in the microwave and stared at the oven's lit-up door.

"Does Taylor know?" I asked.

"He must have guessed by now. He's absentminded but he's not stupid."

I realized for the first time in at least a year that America had thrown me again. There was no word I could learn, no one I could consult, to understand what Wylie was saying or why she had done it. She wasn't happy? She looked happy, sounded happy, acted happy. Then what did happy mean? Her only chance? Happiness was so narrow a door, so selective? The microwave pinged its readiness, and I started crying for my own helplessness and stupidity, but Wylie grabbed me and hugged and started crying herself, telling me it was okay, I would stay on here with Duff and Taylor; Taylor loved me and needed me, needed me even more now that there was Stuart. She said she needed me, too, and on weekends or whenever they arranged Duff's visits, I'd go to her with Duff. They weren't about to abandon me.

"We love you," Wylie said, simply.

I crushed my face into her sweatshirt. If I let go of her, I'd be losing everything.

"Taylor loves you," Wylie said, "but you must know that."

"Don't go," I begged. "Don't leave. Please." What was it that Taylor had explained about weak gravity? Bat-winged nightmares flapped frantically; I didn't want them flying out of my skull.

Two weeks later Wylie left, for Paris. She let Taylor think she might be back, might not. He asked what I thought. What are the odds on four years and a kid together lasting into five or ten? He acted forbearing even when aggrieved. Prakash would have slugged and raved. Prakash would have been impossibly possessive. He would have put in new locks and bars on the *outside* of the front door to the apartment. The Claremont codes still bewildered me.

The odds on Wylie coming home again were nonexistent, but I didn't tell Taylor. Wylie'd confided before she left that Stuart was joining her. Ten glorious days without children on the Continent.

"It'll be okay," I comforted Taylor. "Everything'll be okay. Wait and see."

Taylor let himself be comforted. "It won't be okay by itself. But you'll make it okay, Jase. If you hadn't been here, I'd have gone crazy."

Maybe Wylie, who could see more clearly into people's hearts than I did, was right. Maybe Taylor *was* very fond of me. Even a little bit in love with me. But in love with me in a different way than he was in love with witty, confident Wylie. On the nights that he had time to help tuck Duff in bed—a ritual that Wylie'd cherished—he wanted me to stay in the darkened room, to sit on my cot with him so he could lay one of his big pale hands on Duff's and the other on mine and spin long bedtime stories about the muddles and mysteries of physics. On those nights, we—Duff, Taylor, and I—became a small, self-sufficient family, and I told myself, guiltily, that everything might really work out all right. I prayed that Wylie and Stuart would take all the time they needed in Europe, because I, the caregiver, was eager to lavish care on my new, perfect family.

Wylie'd wanted me to meet Stuart, and so I did. I think now that in the smart magazines that she read there were probably articles on the dos and don'ts for introducing your live-in caregiver to your live-out lover. Claremont Avenue was a brave new world for me. Our first meeting was in Stuart's apartment, and I know I acted awkward and bashfully formal. Stuart was tall and pleasant and extremely thin. He ran six miles a day along Riverside Drive—he'd even noticed Duff and me playing in the park. He had been to India several times as a guest lecturer in Delhi, as a World Bank consultant, as a U.S. government aid officer. He spoke Hindi passably and owned so many Indian paintings and tapestries that his living room looked to me like a shop or an art gallery. His wife was an Africa specialist, so the walls were hung with spears and masks that competed with mirror-work cloths and Moghul miniatures. Their three sons were in private schools in Massachusetts. If there had been no Taylor, Stuart would have been perfect. Knowing Taylor, I found Stuart too secure, too vain, too solicitous.

I carried on. So did Taylor, who sunk himself in his lab and made sure he was always home at the right hour for Duff's dinner and bedtime. Though Taylor's grin had stiffened into a pained and patient smile, he didn't seem bitter about the reduced size of the family. The truth is, we were happy, happier than when Wylie'd been around filling up the apartment with her restlessness and unspoken guilt. Now the rooms seemed warmed by a mute intimacy. My life had a new fullness and chargedness to it. Every day I made discoveries about the city, and in the evenings, when I listed my discoveries to Taylor he listened carefully, as though I were describing an unmapped, exotic metropolis.

Wylie, too, would have been proud of me. I took Duff to the Asia Society to watch an Indian potter. I took her to a fishmonger's display window on Broadway, so she could see fish dressed in leather ties and dark glasses to look like rock stars. I asked Duff the enriching questions Wylie wanted me to, and let Duff find the answers for herself. I wondered if anyone had asked Wylie enriching questions, if I was creating the foundations for impossible yearning later in Duff's life. We rode the buses up and down and across our frantic borough to the Muzak of "And what do you call that, sweetheart?" and "Where did we see it before? Did it look different yesterday?"

Taylor took us to Mets games. Only the National League, he said. We don't do DH. In his growing up in an academic family, there was a secular trinity: NBC, the National League, and the Democratic Party. Anything else was reactionary, racist, anti-intellectual. But when I told Wylie about the trinity, she hooted, What about Edward R. Murrow? Wylie's point was that teaching me baseball was Taylor's unthreatening way of courting me. Maybe. At the time I thought he was consoling himself with teaching me.

Taylor didn't want to change me. He didn't want to scour and sanitize the foreignness. My being different from Wylie or Kate didn't scare him. I changed because I wanted to. To bunker oneself inside nostalgia, to sheathe the heart in a bulletproof vest, was to be a coward. On Claremont Avenue, in the Hayeses' big, clean, brightly lit apartment, I bloomed from a diffident alien with forged documents into adventurous Jase.

In the first weeks of my adventurousness, when Duff and I decided we'd like some of the merchandise advertised on television, I sent away for it. First came a Japanese knife set. Then a radio-controlled Lamborghini. A cassette car stereo for the car I meant to buy someday. A triple-beveled, herringbone, 14-carat-gold neck chain. By the time a spring mechanism for doing sit-ups arrived, I'd grown afraid of the mail. The mailman was a terrorist delivering small explosive objects that wouldn't go away, every month new classical recordings and new history books. I was turning over my entire paycheck for things I couldn't use and didn't know how to stop.

Taylor rescued me. "America, America!" Taylor said one day. Duff probably told him that I was afraid to go outside. He wrote on a package in thick marking pen RETURN TO SENDER. That's all you need to do, he explained. If something gets too frightening, just pull down an imaginary shade that says RETURN on it and you can make it go away.

Could I really have not known that I was head over heels in love with Taylor Hayes?

One Sunday we took our supper in a basket to the park. Duff rolled on the grass. "I'm a puppy," she squealed. "Tickle me behind the ears. Pick me up by my scruff." Taylor and I tickled; then Taylor, too, rolled over on the grass.

"Jase," he said.

He was licking the last of the mango pickle off his fingers. "What would it take to make you stay on?"

"If Duff needs me, I'll stay."

"Sure Duff needs you. That's pretty obvious." We each had our hands on her, idly tickling.

"I want a hot dog," she said. "There's a man over there."

Taylor peeled off a dollar and sent her on her way.

"I think maybe I need you," he said. He scrambled for my hand. "I know you think that Wylie is terrible for walking out—"

I started to protest.

"—but that's not the whole story. She was on to something I wasn't even aware of."

He reached for my hand. "She said I've been in love with you since the first morning I saw you. Since you came in afraid to talk, not knowing much English . . ."

". . . afraid to sleep alone," I said. I did not want this conversation to end. It was not like the businessman who wanted to take me with him to India, who would have paid me thousands. Not like the men in shops along Broadway, the doormen and the street vendors and the repairmen who knew I was a day mummy and fundamentally helpless, or at least available. This was a man I had observed for over two years, who had been unfailingly kind, never condescending, always proud of my achievements. I would listen. And then I would do. I twisted over to keep an eye on Duff, who was already coming back to us, hot dog in her hand.

"Ah, about this sleeping-alone stuff," he said. "Jase? Jase—you listening?"

I acted annoyed. "When have I not listened?"

Duff offered a bite of her hot dog first to Taylor, then to me. She was an instinctively generous, loving child. If we could have stayed like that forever, my world would have righted itself. Fishermen wouldn't have needed their fish.

"You know what the hot-dog man said?" asked Duff. "He asked me, 'Is that lady your mummy?' "

Taylor laughed. I squinted across the open field where children were playing whiffle ball, to the dark-skinned hot-dog vendor sitting under his umbrella.

"Jase? What's wrong? You're shivering. It's something I said, isn't it? Jase, I'm sorry, I'm sorry."

He pulled me to my feet and I couldn't let go of him. I couldn't look behind me, couldn't open my eyes. I could hear Taylor's voice from a long way off saying, *It's okay, she choked on something, she'll be all right.*

He was walking me now, half-pulling me, back to the cement benches that lined the mall. I could feel Duff reaching for my hand. I wanted to talk, but my throat had sealed. I couldn't get my breath, it was like asthma.

We were standing by the traffic light at Ninety-sixth Street, at the bottom of Riverside Drive's longest hill. "Tell me what's wrong, for god's sake. Can I get you anything?"

"That was the man who killed my husband," I said, between long gasps. "He knows . . . he knows me. He knows I'm here."

188

"For god's sake, we'll call the cops," said Taylor. He was shaken. I told him everything: the marriage, the bombing, the murder. I had been until that time an innocent child he'd picked out of the gutter, discovered, and made whole, then fallen in love with.

"Don't you see that's impossible? I'm illegal here, he knows that. I can't come out and challenge him. I'm very exposed, I'm alone all day, I'm out in the park—" I remembered Wylie's Stuart having observed me for months, and suddenly I felt filthy, having been observed, tracked, by Sukhwinder.

"New York's huge. We can move downtown, go to Jersey—"

"This isn't your battle. He'd kill you, or Duff, to get at me."

In my life, I have never dithered. God's plans have always seemed clearly laid out. I said to him, "I'm going to Iowa."

He said I was crazy to leave New York. Iowa was for little old ladies in tennis shoes and for high-school girls in trouble. He said if ghosts were scaring me, he was the best ghostbuster available.

"Iowa? You can't go to Iowa—Iowa's flat."

24

HARLAN KROENER shot Bud on December 23, two years ago. Du had been with us for about eleven months, but this was his first real American Christmas and we'd tried to make it special. Bud, of course, was a traditionalist who'd gotten away from it after his sons were grown. He was back into it in a big way. He'd even wanted to get a model train, but didn't have time to set it up.

We had each given Du as many presents as a large tree could shelter, making up for all his missed Christmases past. I was a veteran of American Christmases, since Taylor and Wylie were aggressive sentimentalists, for Duff's sake, they said, but really because they'd both come from traditional American families, where a Christmas goose was cooked, presents wrapped, family ornaments packed in protective paper all year, and nothing opened until Christmas morning. They loved to go caroling, holding candles and singing their way down Claremont Avenue. In the Christmas season, New York became just another small town for them, like Taylor's upstate New York and Wylie's Maryland. They took me to the midnight church services, and the weekend trips upstate for skiing and sleigh rides.

I was stooped under the large tree in the corner of the living room, sweeping pine needles off the presents and the white sheet that was supposed to be snow, when I heard the whomp of a heavy man's winter boots on the front steps which Bud had just been shoveling. In fact, I thought it was Bud coming back.

When I turned, straightening up, to see who it was—why shouldn't I have hoped that it was the UPS man bringing me a gift from Taylor and Duff, or maybe Wylie and Stuart, or even another pair of knitted pink wool slippers from Lillian Gordon?—there was Harlan Kroener filling the front door. I'd seen the rifle under his coat, but I hadn't thought it strange. Well, strange, yes. I've gone through this moment a thousand times. Is it the wife's job to sort out possible assassins?

When the police came round I said yes, I had seen the rifle. And I'd thought, Shouldn't he be leaving it in his truck? But in those days Bud didn't talk to me about his problems, or the bank's problems. The name Harlan Kroener wasn't red-flagged in any way. And Bud's shooting was the first. There'd been some suicides, but never a murder attempt. So Harlan didn't register on me as a disturbed and violent farmer who saw himself betrayed by his banker. And no, he didn't manifest any signs of violence, except for the flat authority of his voice. I should know these things—I know them now. The inexpressive voice comes from a demented man. Flat affect is the sign of murderous rage. Learn to read the world and everyone in it like a photographic negative of reality.

"Where's Bud?" He said that very quietly. "I'm going to take him with me." I'd been in Baden less than two years, and though Bud made me feel that without my typing and filing the bank would collapse, I hadn't caught on to how tense November and December are for the Ag Loans men.

For every banker who can't overderelict, there's a farmer who can't keep up his payments. "Bud," I called out, "there's someone here to see you."

I delivered him to his crippler. Bud was still in his jacket and boots. He'd been in the shed, tinkering with the snowblower. Even a banker is still a farmer at heart.

Bud was such a big, hearty man. He was fifty-three, but I couldn't calculate the thirty years between us even as a gap, as an October-May kind of thing. He was so fit, so determined to remain fit. He'd quit smoking. He cross-country skied and tried to get me started. In the summer he played tennis and racquetball. He said he'd made his adjustments to the eighties, to cutting back from all the things that spelled manhood to his father's generation.

"Harlan," he said real evenly, "how nice to see you.

Won't you come into the kitchen? Have some coffee, take off your coat—"

"Banker," Harlan said, the way you might say "Reverend" or "Professor." "Banker, I don't reckon you and me's got a whole lot to talk about."

"Honey, you might want to ring up Jimmy Yoder," said Bud, in that same friendly way of his, but I was rearranging the Christmas gifts under the tree and I didn't understand why I should call the ineffectual sheriff that Bud was always complaining about when I had plenty of other things to do right here in the living room. "Soon as I get this done," I said.

"That's a nice tree, Banker. Lots of nice presents. And that's your new little wife, ain't it? Real pretty. Real nice, warm, comfy home, too."

"Where'd you have in mind us going, Harlan?"

"Oh, maybe just driving. Maybe over t'my place. I'd like to show you my Christmas tree and the presents I'm getting my wife and kids."

"What say I come by tomorrow?"

"I say now, Banker."

"Sure thing, Harlan. Honey, we're going over to Harlan Kroener's, case Jimmy Yoder asks. Got that?"

When he kissed me, there by the tree, he whispered something in my ear that I wasn't expecting and so didn't catch. Now of course I know: *He's going to shoot me*, and he gave me a fierce hand pull that made me flinch.

If Du had been in the room too, he would have heard Bud's whisper. Du would have known what to do. He would have saved Bud. But he was in his own room. I could hear his television going.

A couple of weeks ago, when Bud was in Des Moines for a conference, a strange man drove into our yard in a dusty Eldorado. I watched him from behind the kitchen curtain. He got out and looked over at the abandoned harrow with the rusty disks and tines, the barn with the caved-in roof, the empty silo. He didn't look any different from the men in Elsa County; he had their same tumbling walk and fairness and thick-bodiedness. He might have stopped at Earnie's Tavern up the road.

I opened the back door before he could knock. It was cool out. The moon was a pale half-pie in the clear sky. It didn't look or feel like evening yet. Peril felt on hold.

"Your husband at home?" The man distractedly rubbed a denim sleeve up his muscled forearm. I made out a two-color tattoo.

"Not yet." My voice suggested I had a protector who was gunning his pickup home, that very minute.

"I'll come back, then. I have some information to relay to rural folk."

"Who should I say stopped by?"

"I'll be back. My instructions are to read this to the whole family at one time." He didn't show me any brochure.

I watched the Eldorado with Nebraska plates pull out and take the road to Darrel's, real slow.

Du called from his room. "Was that the guy with important information to lay on rural folk? Did he refuse to tell you anything?"

"That's the man, Du."

"He must think there are weird people in this house." He came out, looking a little worried.

"Weird? The weird man thinks we're weird?"

"Well, look at it his way. First time he comes, he gets me. Second time he gets you. Just think what kind of father he expects."

A little later, I called Darrel. "Did you have a visitor?" I asked.

"No," Darrel said. I heard corn popping on the stove. "Probably a poor fellow selling insurance. Relax, Harlan's dead. That business is over for good."

"Okay, I'm taking your advice. Maybe he's a concerned environmentalist."

Du picked up his extension. "Did he call this place 'a federal post'? Did he say organic law transcends man's law? Did he talk about the international banking conspiracy?"

"Stop it!" I'd never heard Darrel that angry. "You scare your mother one more time and I'll come over and personally thrash you one."

Karin, Bud's ex, once called me a gold digger. We were in front of the frozen-foods section of the Hy-Vee. I was embarrassed that she'd caught me reaching for an apple pie. She must have baked them from scratch for Bud. Her cart was stacked neat with Weight Watchers frozen dinners. She, too, was planning changes. Bud *is* gold, I retorted, and if digging him out of the sadness he was in when I met him was what she meant, then, yes, I was a gold digger.

Karin might have talked Harlan into handing over the rifle. She runs counseling sessions in church basements. Get your hate out into the open, she tells troubled men. Make a banker doll out of papier-mâché and bury it in a hole in your garden.

That first fall I was so busy loving Bud and settling Du in school and fighting off Karin that I missed what was happening between Bud and Harlan. I thought of Bud as a secular god of Baden, and everyone in town as his devotee. Shooting Bud was unthinkable, a deicide, worse than assassinating the Mahatma.

Mother Ripplemeyer got me the job in the bank. I met her in the Personnel Office of the University Hospital. One minute I was begging a potato-faced woman behind the widest, cleanest counter for a job, any job (telling her that I would do whatever needed doing, the psychiatric ward, the deathwatch, anything, because I was desperate and I didn't know anyone in Iowa), and the next minute a woman with the curtness and directness of Lillian Gordon, only older, tapped me on the shoulder and said, "You need a meal as well as a job, dear. I'm going to take you home for lunch; then I'm going to call Bud and see if he doesn't need a pretty new teller."

Lillian Gordon, Mother Ripplemeyer: one day I want to belong to that tribe.

Wednesdays are Mother's days to help out in the gift shop in the hospital lobby and to have lunch with Mrs. Bloomquist, the potato-faced woman, in the staff cafeteria. If I'd begged Mrs. Bloomquist on any day other than a Wednesday, my life would have skidded to a different groove.

A crazy kind of logic made me pick Iowa to run away to. Duff's mother had had Duff, Wylie'd told me, at an Elsa County hospital. Duff, conceived in impulse and error, had given her mother a chance to go to college and me the chance to break out of Flushing. Iowa was a state where miracles still happened.

Taylor, who didn't believe in miracles, wanted me to stay, at least until Wylie had decided between lover and husband. Then he would decide between Wylie and separation. Duff was in bed in the room that she and I shared, and Wylie was in Frankfurt. "Sleep with me tonight," Taylor whispered. "Jase, please."

I have had a husband for each of the women I have been. Prakash for Jasmine, Taylor for Jase, Bud for Jane. Half-Face for Kali.

*   *   *

I am leading Taylor to a bed as wide as a subcontinent, I am laying my cheek on his warm cheek, I am closing his eyes with my caregiving fingertips, I am tucking the mosquito netting tight under his and Wylie's king-sized mattress. He is snoring soft, happy, whispery snores of a sleeper safe from Sukkhi and Half-Face, from nothing more horrible than Stuart Eschelman.

Stop!
It's Bud who tries to make me happy now.

Bud says he knew he shouldn't have walked in *front* of Harlan. I didn't know it then, but Harlan'd parked his pickup a hundred yards up the highway from us. He should have parked in our driveway, but he didn't. Karin would have read the signals: a man does the least little thing out of the ordinary and he's planning. If he had kept Harlan in front of him, he could have reacted in time. He was stupid, believing in John Wayne bravery and codes of Hollywood honor. Good men might weaken and get pushed to the brink, but they would never, never shoot their targets in the back. If I keep him behind me, I'll be all right, he thought.

Harlan shot Bud twice in the back as Bud was reaching for the door handle on the passenger side. Shot in the *cauda equina*, the doctor at the University Hospital explained to me, resting his wide, firm palm in the middle part of my lower back. And because I was stunned I said,

"*Cauda equina?* Masterji didn't teach me that word." The
doctor gave me Valium.

After Harlan shot Bud, he blew his own head off. It was
Du who came out of his room and said, "What was that?
Sounded like a rifle." I'd heard nothing. We listened; we
heard the prairie wind between the windows. Du, again,
half an hour later, heard one long scream, like the screams
he remembered of a man in agony. He called the police.

Shoveling the snow off the porch was the last free-
standing task Bud ever performed. His last able-bodied act.
How I used to hate to shovel! he says now.

Bud says that when Mother called him and told him that
she was sending over a starving Indian to save he'd pictured
a stick-legged, potbellied, veiled dark woman like the ones
he'd seen fleeing wars, floods, and famines on television.

He says, *I saw you walk in and I felt my life was just
opening to me. Like a door had just been opened. There you
were in my bank, and I couldn't believe it. It felt as if I was
a child again, back in the Saturday-afternoon movies. You
were glamour, something unattainable. And you were
standing there with my mother.*

"So you wouldn't have hired me if I hadn't been pretty?"
I'm teasing. It's a cherished routine.

"No, no." He grins. "I'm a good Lutheran. I might have
hired you, but I wouldn't have asked you to lunch."

Banking in Baden is intuitive. You know in your gut whom to carry and whom to foreclose. He saw me lope in, frightened, jobless, less than a month from New York, and he knew right away that he wanted me more than he'd ever wanted anyone. "Jane," he likes to say, nuzzling his head between my breasts, "you brought me back from the dead."

To want anything so much, I wanted to tell him then, was unwise. Too much attachment, too much disillusion.

"I brought you back from a mid-life crisis, don't exaggerate," I tease. "I have good timing."

Bud courts me because I am alien. I am darkness, mystery, inscrutability. The East plugs me into instant vitality and wisdom. I rejuvenate him simply by being who I am.

Bud would have left Karin, or twisted in mid-life until he dropped. I was a catalyst, not a cause. I make him feel what he's never felt, do what he's never done. There's a shape-changing, risk-taking pirate rattling the cage of his heavy flesh. Baden was death until you came, he tells me, you brought me back from the dead. "Rubbish!" I tell him lightly. "I'm a passive person. I've done no saving of any kind."

I did watch him, the pillar of Baden, punch a drunk once. It happened at Earnie's, the bar six miles on the road to Dalton. A big, dusty, blond man was having a drink at the counter with a sad-looking older man. They looked as if they were trying to wipe out the last three or four years of drought or depression in one dedicated night. When we passed them on our way to the nearest empty booth, they didn't wave to Bud, so I knew they didn't borrow from our bank. The older man was boasting about some new research on EPDs that was about to take all risk out of buying bulls and make him a rich man. The younger man managed a wheezy laugh. "Did you see what I just seen? Can you believe that?"

"*Estimated Progeny Differences*," said the older man. "A professor's working out the horsepower of bulls."

"Shit, that fucker must be older'n you, Woody. Where's he get off?" That's when the younger man gave his bar stool a noisy twirl and fixed on me. "Whoa! I don't know nothing about horsepower, but I know *whore*power when I see it!" His next words were in something foreign, but probably Japanese or Thai or Filipino, something bar girls responded to in places where he'd spent his rifle-toting youth.

I wish I'd known America before it got perverted.

But Bud smashed his cigarette out in the tinfoil ashtray, lumbered over to the twirling man, and knocked his head back with a soft, clumsy punch.

Gold digger and Lazarus.

The Sunday after Bud left her, Karin stalked me all morning at the fair the Mennonites put on for their Relief Fund. The Mennonites were raising money for camps full of starving Ethiopians. Women in gauzy white caps smiled encouragingly at me. Every quilt auctioned, every jar of apple butter licked clean had helped somebody like me.

She said, "I'm ashamed of something I did yesterday."

We were in a large, stuffy shed pretending to examine Depression glass, centennial plates, miniature wind-mills, and used toys that would later be auctioned. I said, "You don't have to tell me, Karin. And I don't have to listen."

There was misery in her muddy blue eyes. "I wrote your name on a piece of paper. Then I lit it with a match."

I rocked the hand-carved rocking horses, and spun the tiny wheels of model trains. There was a model tractor commemorating John Deere's fortieth anniversary. All the dolls had yellow hair. It had been a simpler America. The toys weren't unusual or valuable; they were shabby, an ordinary family's cared-for memorabilia. Bud's generic past crowded the display tables. I felt too exotic, too alien.

Karin went on: "I feel hate for you. I want to be a good Christian."

I moved out of the shed. A Mennonite girl, her lace cap riding the waves in her golden hair like a skiff, was holding a puppy with a price tag hanging from its collar. The girl crushed her face into the puppy's. I hated her having to give up the puppy, even if it was to help starving Ethi-opians.

"Help me," Karin said.

The sky, softened by summer heat, puffed out over the treeless fairground.

"Help me not to hate you, Jasmine."

Around us big men in overalls lined up for the $4.75 buffet breakfast. Eggs, sausages, pancakes, home-baked breads and coffee cakes, jams and apple butter, cantaloupes, strawberries, and melons. Mennonite teenagers raced sedately in polished Model T's. Somber children stood in line for pony rides. The astrologer of Hasnapur cackled his predictions over the cheery noises of the fairgrounds: foolish and wicked girl, did I not tell you you'd end up among aliens?

"Forgiving's going to take me the rest of my life, but I'm going to do it."

Sukkhi, the New York vendor, pushes his hot-dog cart through my head. I do not seek to forgive, and I have long let go of my plans for revenge. I can live with both impulses. I have even written an anonymous letter to the INS, suggesting they look into the status of a certain Sukhwinder Singh, who pushes a hot-dog cart in New York City. Goodness and evil square off every moment. Forgiveness implies belief in an ultimate triumph. I dream only of neutralizing harm, not absolute and permanent conquest.

"I might leave here," Karin continued. We'd made our grim way into the cool, dark shed where quilts were being displayed. One hundred and seven pieces, numbered and encased in clear plastic, hung from rods.

"You've been here just months and you've managed to drive me out of Baden." She kicked up a forlorn cloud of sawdust with her navy flats.

"Bud's happy," I said. "I didn't do anything to make him

happy, but he's happy. Does that help?" I walked away toward a quilt that seemed not exotic but different, among the traditional Mennonite pieces. This one—smoky blue whorls swirling seamlessly on a sky of slate gray—intrigued me because of the invisibility of its quilting stitches. I read the card stapled to it: The Lutheran (Hmong) Church of Dalton. The Hmong, too, had fled. In Dalton, where fast-talking developers were planning their buyout of Darrel, Hmong women, animists and Lutheran, were quilting in church basements.

"Maybe I'll go off to L.A. Half of Iowa's relocated to L.A. Maybe this kick in the pants is what I needed. I should be thanking you."

I said, "You don't have to go anywhere."

"Aside from Bud, I've won only one thing in my life. I won a Purple Ribbon in a 4H state fair with my How-to-Pack-a-Suitcase demo," Karin said. She could have been talking to herself. "I could pack the best bag but I never got to travel. Not like you. You travel around the world, swoop down in a small town and take the best man for yourself and don't even think of the pain you've left behind."

"He chose me. I did nothing to encourage it."

"And I suppose you never asked, 'Are you a married man?' You just batted your big black eyes and told him how wonderful he was, didn't you?"

She covered her face with her large-knuckled, middle-aged hands. I watched the disintegration of enviable virtues: dutifulness, decency, compassion. Where could I go?

Karin sobbed. "I have no way of competing with you! Last night I dreamed that Baden was hit by a tornado. I don't have to ask a shrink to know that you are the tornado. You're leaving a path of destruction behind you. I'm going to L.A. where you can't hurt me anymore."

But she didn't run away. She lives alone in the two-story brick-and-wood house with white columns that Bud built for her. It's the kind of large, neat, comfortable house that perfect TV families of the fifties live in, in Du's black-and-white reruns. She invited me in a month after she had told me her tornado dream. By then she'd accepted the change, she said. She still had her health, her friends. It wasn't the end of the world. Even in Elsa County there was a high percentage of divorces, and getting higher. She was the norm.

She'd been tidying up the storage area of the basement and found some things of Bud's that she thought I might want. She had them in a shopping sack: a red satin windbreaker with BADEN LANES embroidered in yellow silk on the back, and a pair of freshly polished bowling shoes. Bud wears size 10. In the car I put on Bud's bowling jacket over my cotton blouse. But the bowling shoes with the number 10 on the heel made me shudder so much that I dumped Bud's shoes in Karin's trash can.

Karin found herself a volunteer job right after the divorce. She staffs the only Suicide Hot Line in the county. When Bud was shot two years ago, I saw her on television. She said, "It doesn't have to be war out there, that's what I tell the men who call. They aren't bad managers. Farming isn't a business you manage between nine and five like an office job. It's a way of life. I find myself talking to frightened, panicked people, to angry people who don't know whom to be angry at. The banker just happens to be visible."

If she had been in the house when Harlan broke into our living room, she would have known what to do. I feel responsible. For Prakash's death, Bud's maiming. I'm a tornado, blowing through Baden.

Karin and I have had just one other confrontation. Yesterday she called me and said, "I thought I was doing okay until I heard you were pregnant. Why? Why are you forcing a man in Bud's condition to go through with this? What do you know about looking after a man like Bud? What are you trying to prove? He already has two good, affectionate sons."

I said, "Karin, maybe you ought to write my name on a slip of paper and burn it again."

For seconds I heard nothing, as though Karin's phone had gone dead. "Hullo, Karin?" I shouted. Screams, taunts, meanness would have been easier for me to fight. "Hullo! Hullo!" Then soft, raspy noises floated at me. I could picture Karin by the telephone table in the hallway of her big house, twisting and twisting the telephone cord around her wrist. I thought I heard the sighs of a wild, despairing woman. "Karin," I pleaded, "I'm not the enemy."

A sigh thickened into a gravelly cough. Finally Karin said, "How's the Lutz boy doing out there alone? I worry about him. He used to call me a lot, but he doesn't call me much anymore."

"Hey, I may have one more for you," Thad, the mail-man, shouts as he is about to get back into his funny little mail jeep. Some days he parks just outside our driveway and eats his lunch in the jeep. One time he broke his thermos and I brought him a mug of microwaved water for his tea bag. He's a friendly, bearded, bookish-looking man who once spent a month in Kathmandu and tries out Nepalese words on me that I don't understand but that I pretend to. He sees himself as the final link in a world of communications. Someone ten thousand miles away drops a letter in a strange-looking box and a week later, out of all the people in the world, it comes to him and he gets to lay it in my hand. (He also said, "If I didn't make up these little stories, I'd go crazy.") He tells me the names of famous people on his route, famous meaning they were in the papers, even the Des Moines *Register*, for winning something, or losing.

I don't think, growing up in Hasnapur, we ever sent or received a letter. I like to keep him talking as long as I can; he brings the world with him, and when he finally drives away, I feel abandoned, almost betrayed. I used to feel so secure, being alone on the farm with Bud, in the winter; now I feel deserted, except for Du, who rarely talks. New York wasn't like this. Even with the men in stores and on the streets, I felt safe and never alone. I think sometimes I can appease the mailman; I see his jeep approaching from a mile away and I say a quick series of prayers, the way I do when a promising cloud appears on the low horizon. *Rain, rain,* I say, the same way I find myself praying, *Letter, letter, from New York.* I think sometimes if I can come up with the right prayer or appeasement, a letter will come from New York. Taylor will find me somehow, sometime.

"If it's a bill, I don't need it." I laugh, but I take the kitchen steps in one running leap. I don't get or send out much mail, I rip myself free of the past. Why leave a paper trail for the INS to track? Only this noon, what the mailman's holding in his hand is not a glassine envelope but a black-and-white postcard with a woman's face on it. The woman has stark-white bobbed hair and a sad, heavy, wrinkled face. It's the face of a poet or a philosopher, the face of a woman who has come to terms with all the Sukkhis and Half-Faces out there and is no longer afraid.

"Hold on, Mrs. R.," he says, squinting at the address. "I figure around here you're the only one with a name like this." He mouths the name on the postcard to himself.

I read his lips, I hold my breath. "Jasmine Vijh, yes."

"Oh, jeez," he says, handing over the card. "Is that Jane in Hindu? Sure sounds prettier in your language." It's addressed to Jasmine Vijh, Elsa County, Iowa, and it's found me here. Less than a week old.

"Hindi," I say.

The card says: DUFF AND I'RE HEADING YOUR WAY. SHE STILL DOESN'T KNOW AND I'M HOPING YOU'LL HELP.

JASMINE

SHE'S QUITE A YOUNG LADY AND SHE REMEMBERS YOU
PERFECTLY. AS DO I. WYLIE DOESN'T CONSIDER MY TRIP
INSANE. STAY PUT. DON'T DARE RUN AWAY AGAIN. ??? T.

Is the word before *T* "love"? I lean against the cold dusty
side of the jeep in case my legs give way. How bold to
scribble "love" on a postcard that anyone can read, how
lucky to be a man without secrets.

Du is standing by the fridge drinking 2 percent milk
straight out of the carton. We can't get him to drink skim.
"Don't worry," he says, not looking at me, "I'm not watching you."

"What *are* you watching, then?"

"Whatever you're planning to do is okay. Just do it." His
eyes fix on the postcard on top of the fridge. I haven't
hidden Taylor's postcard. It's easy to hide things from a
man in a wheelchair.

"Do I look as though I'm plotting?"

"So now you want me to look at you?"

"Didn't anyone ever teach you to pour milk into a glass
first?"

"I went to a cheap manners school, remember? Anyway,
even if I did, would that make Dad love me any more?"

"He's a good father, Du. Don't take that away from
him."

"Okay, he's a good father. He gives us a good home."

How dare we want more? I march to the window and
bang it down to the sill. The glass is cold. Coldness,

darkness swirl outdoors. I try to garrison myself with light, with warmth. Out there somewhere Taylor and Duff are burning up the highways. They point their car onto the West Side Highway, then take the exit to the George Washington Bridge, and without another traffic light, they end up in Elsa County, Iowa, like a letter.

"Who's your Mr. T.?" Du asks, very cautiously. "Gold chains and a Mohawk?"

"Mr. T!" I touch Du's receding hair with the fluttery tips of my fingers. What crazy connections he makes—Taylor and Mr. T. I want to tell him something he may never have learned: Don't get too close to Mr. T. Mr. T. is the enemy. The whole A-Team, they're the assholes. America keeps sending these ambiguous messages. "I looked after their little girl, that's all. I already told you about him."

He puts the carton back. He looks at me and I can read his mind: *And whose little boy am I?* From the hallway I hear him one more time. "By the way, you know who that woman is on the postcard?"

Du never asks a question unless he already knows the answer. He asks only to test us.

"Go ahead, tell me."

"A revolutionary's wife who ended up living among strangers." His door, wired with electronic gadgets, whirs shut. The name on the postcard, British-born, married to a Russian, means nothing to me.

My wise son wants me to do the right thing.

Taylor the Rescuer is on his way here. He taught me to yank down that window shade. For a couple of years I felt powerful, shutting out meanness and sealing in goodness. Then I saw Sukkhi that day in the park and it was as though the cord came off in my hand.

On Claremont Avenue I came closest to the headiness, dizziness, *porousness* of my days with Prakash. What I feel for Bud is affection. Duty and prudence count. Bud has kept me out of trouble. I don't want trouble. Taylor's car is gobbling up the highways.

25

Bud's working late tonight because the team of state inspectors is due next week. He used to welcome them. He called it his private seminar in ag banking. They used to come every year and a half and spend a week at the bank, inspecting each loan, commenting on its riskiness, raising routine doubts about collateral. Bud enjoyed the give-and-take. His faith in character, integrity, and the basic soundness of an operation, against their charts and statistics. He always won.

Now their load's so heavy they don't come that often, and it's become impersonal. Cranky bureaucrats, men with itchy collars and high-pitched voices, suggesting that *this* looks like a bad loan, and this and this, saying in pained voices that a banker who co-signs his neighbor's loan—which Bud'd often done for Gene Lutz and which he, now, torments himself thinking he should do for Darrel—is getting that farmer in a tougher spot than if he were to point out in a no-options voice, "No way you can make all these payments." In these times a good banker has to be able to walk away from dreamers and pleaders and potential defaulters.

"I'll wait supper for you. Indian wives never eat before their husbands." I add a laugh to lighten what I've just said.

Bud cries, "Wife? Did I hear wife?"

There's so much about me he doesn't know, that might kill him to find out. The old Bud, the pre-Harlan Bud, I might have been able to tell. And then marry.

"Marry me, Jane," the pillar of Baden begs. I hear Orrin Lacey saying, Look, Bud, this is his situation. We'll have to tell him, let's look at what's best for you. You still have $200,000. Now let's figure out what's the most essential part of your operation, and see if you shouldn't sell off eighty acres. Orrin must be picking at his graying sixties sideburns or at his droopy mustache. He does that when he has to deliver unpleasant news.

"Marry me before the baby comes. Put this old bull out of his pain."

I stick the pot roast back in the oven. Pot roast and gobi aloo: sacrilegious smells fill my kitchen. Du is at soccer practice. He'll drive over to Arby's afterward. He passed his driving test on the first try. Amazing, the instructor said.

Only the farm kids who've driven tractors since they were six pass on the first shot. *Why shouldn't he?* I wanted to say. I passed mine; it runs in the family.

At school they say Du's doing so well, isn't he, considering. *Considering what?* I want to say. Considering that he has lived through five or six languages, five or six countries, two or three centuries of history; has seen his country, city, and family butchered, bargained with pirates and bureaucrats, eaten filth in order to stay alive; that he has survived every degradation known to this century, *considering all those liabilities*, isn't it amazing that he can read a Condensed and Simplified for Modern Students edition of *A Tale of Two Cities?*

Du's doing well because he has always trained with live ammo, without a net, with no multiple choice. No guesswork: only certain knowledge or silence. Once upon a time, like me, he was someone else. We've been many selves. We've survived hideous times. I envy Bud the straight lines and smooth planes of his history.

Until Harlan. Always, until Harlan.

"I feel crazy tonight," Darrel says on the phone.

I've called him, after talking to Karin. It's seven-thirty. He should be working on his hog house before the light goes. "How crazy?"

He whistles a song I don't recognize. "Crazy enough to hold up a bank, for instance."

"Stop right there."

"Hijack a school bus. Take hostages. I feel ready for massacre and mayhem."

"Tried calling Karin's Hot Line?"

"Karin'll get her chance if you fail. I'm giving you the chance to save me first."

I still think of myself as caregiver, recipe giver, preserver. I can honestly say all I wanted was to serve, be allowed to join, but I have created confusion and destruction wherever I go. As Karin says, I am a tornado. I hit the trailer parks first, the prefabs, the weakest links. How many more shapes are in me, how many more selves, how many more husbands?

"Come over and say a mantra," Darrel goes on. "Hold my hand. Keep me sane. And if *that* doesn't work, dial Karin."

Karin and Jane, wives of the wounded god. Who will say a mantra for us?

I smell the cumin, coriander, and turmeric even before I push Darrel's back door open. We don't lock, though we should. After three years in Iowa, I still take Manhattan security as the norm. I never belittled Taylor and Wylie's three locks with three separate keys. Many things, even disparate things, are reminding me of Taylor. Has he found Duff another day mummy, a Letitia, some Caribbean make-over to replace his Jase? I whisper the name, Jase, Jase, Jase, as if I am calling someone I once knew.

Darrel stands in the middle of his kitchen, wearing a

butcher's apron and holding a bottle of Bombay lime pickle in a hand that's bleeding from where he cut it on the jagged edge of the bottle's tin cap. Third World packaging.

"Welcome," he announces, and guides me to the kitchen table still cluttered with cereal boxes, dirty mixing bowls, and Baggies of spice.

"I'm ready to serve us a banquet fit for an Indian princess."

"Darrel," I protest, smiling, "I came to save your life, remember? I didn't come to pig out." Bud's and my pot roast is drying in the turned-off oven. A good Hasnapur wife doesn't eat just because she is hungry. Food is a way of granting or withholding love. I lift lids off the two pots on Darrel's stove. He hands me a ladle. "Pilaf," he boasts, "and motor pan. Did I say that right?"

"Does it have peas?" I am dazed by this grown boy's desire to please.

"Yeah," he says, "but I used tofu instead of making the cheese myself. Is that okay?"

"Then it's matar panir," I say. "Matar for peas and panir for cheese." These are errors I feel I can correct.

The rice is crunchy. The tofu has crumbled. The spices sludge up the bottom of the pot. That I was prepared for. But Darrel the Romantic who begins to talk to me now is a mystery. He is twenty-three. I've seen him grieve and rage, plant and harvest, and threaten to sell. I've seen him drunk, I've seen him with his girlfriend, his parents, with Bud. I've seen him tending his hogs like a registered nurse. But now he's a shy, would-be lover with a despondent face, holding my hand in so anxious a grip that I think I must pull away before he breaks it. He's a man transformed.

He doesn't want to be tied down to the farm, he doesn't want to live poor and die rich like his father and grandfather, he wants to fly away to Tahiti, to Mars, to the moon, he wants to make love to an Indian princess.

"He doesn't treat *you* right either," Darrel is saying, "he *can't*, can he?" and I am shocked, for this is the first time anyone has dared to mention Bud and sex.

"I'm warning you. Don't say anything more."

"Oh, Juh-ane, come on. I love you and we're in this together. We can leave it together. New Mexico! I can run a Radio Shack in Santa Fe. You think Yogi's the only electrical genius around here? I'll even give him a job. I can make it there." His face is twisted. Hate for Bud, love for me, vast pity for himself. With a bloody hand he's reaching out to grab me. "Juh-ane," he pleads. "I can't make it here. It's sucking my blood. And Bud's the bloodsucker."

His ghastly curry has congealed on my plate. I can't help staring at it, the whole failed, ambitious design of his evening, his life. "You're being stupid. He's a banker who's loaned you thousands of dollars. Of course he wants you to succeed."

"Oh sure." He looks around the kitchen, nodding to an invisible audience able to appreciate the magnitude of my ignorance. He acknowledges their silent applause.

"Good old Bud Ripplemeyer, huh? He comes on as the friend of everybody. But we know something, don't we?"

He seizes my hands. "He's in it with the big banks, isn't he? The Eastern banks, right? They give the orders and he squeezes us, right?"

Suddenly I can read the blown circuitry behind his eyes. Eastern bankers. Organic law. Aryan Nation Brotherhood. I think of the tattooed man, the dusty Eldorado with the Nebraska plates.

"Darrel, they've gotten to you. Like Harlan. All that's crazy."

"*I'm* crazy. That's good. Bud's degenerating right in front of your eyes and you call me crazy! He's sick in the head with jealousy. He's jealous of anyone who can farm, let alone anyone who can *walk*!"

He's let go of my hands, he's standing, he's shouting in his kitchen, knocking against ladles, spilling pots. "You two are a joke all over Elsa County. Those Dalton guys, *they* call you the Odd Couple—"

"Darrel! Shut up!"

I don't wait to hear the rest. I'm out in my Rabbit worried that Bud's gotten home and not found me or Du, worried that the frontier of madness is closer than I guessed. He's standing at the back door, still ranting, "You can run, Jane, but you can't hide from the truth. I'm the truth."

It would not surprise me to see him reach, this very minute, for the shotgun that must be near. I mustn't show my terror, I must pull out gradually, waving. I must not raise the dust between the elders and the maples.

26

W HEN I get back home Du and another boy or man are on the living-room sofa talking in earnest Vietnamese. He doesn't look as though he's just come back from soccer practice. He looks secretive, conspiratorial, excited. The other Vietnamese—he has an ageless, tight-pored face round as a dinner plate and just about as shiny—is wearing white pants with fancy pleats and green leather shoes that you can't buy in any mall around Baden. He's been writing something on a page torn out of a pocket notebook. I can see the wire coil of the notebook sticking out of the pocket of his loose white shirt. The shirt's looseness seems planned, expensive, a style statement from a different time and continent, a different sense of style and manliness.

"Hi, Mom," Du says, finally. He isn't really seeing me. He looks a million miles away. This is the first time I've heard him speak Vietnamese. His first month here he didn't speak when he couldn't find the right English phrases. He's never brought home any Vietnamese kids. I don't know if there are any in his grade. The Hmong kids he treats with contempt. He, a Saigon sophisticate, thinks of them as illiterate mountain people, peasants. The elegant man in white, I worry, is a drug pusher. What could he be writing out for Du—in a script I can't read—with a fountain pen?

"This is John," Du says.

"Pleased to meet you, Mrs. Ripplemeyer." Bud's name is a real test for most Asians. His accent is hard to understand, but his manners are ingratiating. He is out the front door before I can offer him tea and get him to open up about himself.

Du doesn't stick around the living room either.

I put in a call to Karin's Hot Line, but it's busy.

"Come sit with me, Du."

He stops halfway down the hall.

I say, "If Darrel comes over, don't open the door."

"Okay." He turns.

"What was that guy doing? Selling you something?"

"No," Du says. He misses a beat. Then he says, "He was giving me something."

"You know to just say no to anything you shouldn't say yes to, right?"

"Thank you, Nancy Reagan."

"Is John someone you met today?"

"No."

"Is that all you're going to tell me?"

"What do you want to know? I've known him longer than I've known you. I knew him in the camps. Look, can I have five hundred bucks?"

"Very funny."

"I'll settle for three hundred. I'm taking a bus to L.A. to see my sister." He flashes the notepaper with the Vietnamese writing. It's supposed to be an address, his sister's address.

"What sister?"

"I only have one. Left."

The stories of the detention camp flood me. This is the married sister who fed him live worms and lizards and crabs so he wouldn't starve to death.

"I'm leaving for L.A. My sister works in a taco stand. She can look after me, she said. Thank Dad for everything he's done. Tell him I'm sorry." His eyes are glittery with a higher mission. Abandonment, guilt, betrayal: the boy in front of me would consider them banal dilemmas.

"He's got his own kid coming. He never wanted me."

Blood is thick, I think. Du, my adopted son, is a mystery, but the prospect of losing him is like a miscarriage. I had relied on him, my silent ally against the bright lights, the rounded, genial landscape of Iowa. I want to say—to be able to say—you're wrong, Bud loves you, he needs you like I do, but I know Du's right. Du has practiced without a net; he knows his real friends.

"I love you, Du."

I see him duck his head. The perfect young, unblemished face has aged into a hundred jagged cracks. The face is small, wrinkled, old. He runs down the hall, slams his door.

I have never seen him cry.

The line is free. "Karin Ripplemeyer, please. Privately." As briefly as possible I say that I have just come from Darrel Lutz's and I fear for his sanity.

"How do you know?" she demands. I tell her I've seen it. Murder or suicide is a fine line. A good friend of mine, a girl I once knew, has been there.

I am amazed, and a little proud that Du had made a life for himself among the Vietnamese in Baden and I hadn't had a clue. Aside from my Dr. Jaswani and from Dr. Patel in Infertility, I haven't spoken to an Indian since my months in Flushing. My transformation has been genetic; Du's was hyphenated. We were so full of wonder at how fast he became American, but he's a hybrid, like the fantasy appliances he wants to build. His high-school paper did a story on him titled: "Du (Yogi) Ripplemeyer, a Vietnamese-American . . ."

"If you're worried about Darrel hassling you, I can stay till Dad gets back," he says, an hour later. The bag is packed. He moves it from the hall back to his room. "I'm okay," he says.

"It's Dad he wants to get," I say.

He goes to the hall closet, takes down a rifle, loads it, and lays it on my lap. "This isn't a solution," I protest. And darkly, I think it might be. I could pronounce sentence on myself. I could finish off the fates of Du, Bud, and me, all of us marked for death and weirdly spared.

"At least take my car to the airport," I offer.

"It's okay. John's coming for me."

"Write me. Think of me. I'll be thinking of you." I want to say to him, *You were my hero.*

Suddenly I'm bawling. How *dare* he leave me alone out here? How dare he retreat with my admiration, my pride, my total involvement in everything he did? His education was my education. His wirings and circuits were as close to Vijh & Vijh as I would ever get. Perhaps those two drops of soldering were my assignment in this lifetime. Now I could end it.

"At least finish high school," I say. Brusque, maternal.

"L.A. has schools, Mom. And my sister says Cal Tech's a good school."

This time the face is smiling, confident. He's mastered his demons. For the first time in our life together, he bends down, over the rifle, to kiss me. "You gave me a new life. I'll never forget you."

I hear the crunch of gravel. He undoes the lock, announces it's John, not Darrel, not Bud, and on a hot Iowa night, he steps into his future.

I lower myself onto the sofa. Bud has built an ugly, comfortable house. I will be lonely here, with Bud or without him. I can feel the kick of the baby transmitted through the rifle stock.

In Hasnapur Dida told stories of Vishnu the Preserver

containing our world inside his potbellied stomach. I sit, baffled, in the dark living room of our house in Baden, loaded rifle against my belly, cocooning a cosmos.

Half an hour later I am in Du's room, trying to think like Lillian Gordon. She put me on the bus that Florida morning, gave me money and a kiss. She didn't cry, didn't even stay to wave goodbye. I want so much to be like her. Be unsentimental, I order myself. Don't cry, don't feel sorry for yourself; be proud of what we did. He was given to us to save and to strengthen; we didn't own him, his leaving was inevitable. Even healthy.

Had things worked out differently—no Harlan Kroener, no droughts—Du would have had the father of any boy's dream, a funny, generous, impulsive father, an American father from the heartland like the American lover I had for only a year. I would have had a husband, a place to call home.

This, I realize, is not it.

In the America Du knows, mothers are younger than sisters, mothers are illegal aliens, murderers, rape victims; in Du's America, parents are unmarried, fathers are invalids, shot in the back on the eve of Christmas Eve.

Assholes.

He came to sexual awakening outside our bedroom door. No wonder he fled into the silence of circuitry, in crossbreeding appliances, in hoarding and restoring.

I'll leave everything untouched. The drawers full of dead batteries—AA, C, D, E—solar calculators, coffee mugs with men's names (Joe, Bob, Fritz, Al, Vern), new shirts with cardboard still stiffening the collars, immense balls of twine. The electronic chess set stays in the middle of the scatter rug. The Scrabble board sticks out at an angle on the bed, with only two words, "deliquesce" and "scabrous," laid out by imaginary players. He wanted to design computer Scrabble, like computer Chess, a chance for the lonely and word-obsessed to play themselves.

They are clues, but to what? Shadowy road signs for a phantom Columbus? I should have known about his friends, his sister, his community. I should have broken through, but I was afraid to test the delicate thread of his hyphenization. Vietnamese-American: don't question either half too hard. I'm happy that he's visiting his sister. I am not grieving over the loss of a son. His sister kept him alive in the camp; we only gave him tools. From the fields, hidden in the tangles of her ratted hair, she brought him gifts of life, gifts of love: rats, roaches, crabs, snails. For every gesture of loyalty there doesn't have to be a betrayal. The star on my forehead throbs: pain and hope, hope and pain.

I haven't figured out the what and why of Du's hoarding. Or maybe that's the point: exclude no option; someday your life might depend on the length of twine you squirreled away in your desk drawer. But Du's also like me, a striver and a saver, a prudent investor and money manager. I find mail-order catalogues in a language I can't read and a book of order forms. He's been filling out orders for Vietnamese greeting cards—die-cut, stand-up, fold-out beauties. Fish swim across five-panel oceans, birds wing pleated lavender skies. I will keep from Bud the two books of deposit slips stuck inside wool socks we bought him for a Colorado camping trip with Scott and his family. Du was keeping his money in CDs in savings and loans places in Dalton instead of in Bud's bank in Baden. Over two thousand dollars. I am looking at the piggy bank of a new tycoon; also at an insult that Bud would not forgive.

"Bud's not here?" she asks, and I say, "He's still at the bank. Inspectors' visit." She nods. "Of course. How soon we forget." I make her some instant coffee.

The gun is still out, propped by the door. She's too polite to ask me about it.

"I talked to him. He's rambling all over the lot," she says. She's looking around the living room and kitchen, getting her bearings. We bought everything new after the divorce. They look familiar and dingy to me, but for Karin it's a whole new take on Bud. Because of the wheelchair, we keep wide aisles, few tables, no bric-a-brac that he might knock over. The truth is, we're underfurnished, in a meager house.

When she joins me in the kitchen, she sees bottles and tubes of medicine with Bud's name on them; she knows I've been decent in a difficult time. No picnic, is it? she says. Gallon jugs of white vinegar for his soaks: tubes of antibiotics for decubitus ulcers, support hose and diuretics for "dependent" edemas. The keening language, so precise yet so suggestive; blood tests for "occult" presences. Even the bacteria, when they settle in his ulcers, become "indolent."

We've paid a steeper price for our heroic love than even Karin would have set. She picks up a bottle of diuretic medicine, reads the directions. "Otherwise, the fluids gather," I start to explain.

She nods. "I know, I've done some reading. Is he in much pain?" she asks.

"He doesn't complain. But there has to be a lot of pain."

His therapist said amputees sometimes scream from the terrible pain in their absent limbs. It's called phantom pain. Bud will suffer pain from muscle memory; the loss of function, the memory of muscles that have died.

She looks around our living room, at the old pine table and four brightly enameled chairs from an unpainted furniture store, and at the huge wooden Cardinals mascot on a wall. She strokes the scarlet bird. "Did he tell you how he got that silly thing?" she asks, her eyes wet. I nod. He went to St. Louis when they tore down the old stadium. He fought a man for the cardinal. "A man has his obsessions," I say.

Karin paces, picking up things she recognizes, his old ledger books, an old leather-flapped briefcase he'd carried to work for thirty years. When they divorced, Bud packed up his awards, the framed "Man of the Year" citations, the sporting trophies. The cardinal and the citations are now our artwork. He says, What's the use of hanging anything on these walls? Optimistically: we won't be here that long.

Realistically: you can't hang things low enough for me anyway.

"I was wrong to call you a gold digger. I don't know if I could have nursed him."

"We do what we must," I say.

"If you married him for money, you didn't do that great."

"We have enough."

"My lawyer thought you'd adopted that Vietnamese boy in order to raise a big issue in court. Lower the settlement, something like that. I told him it was something Bud was doing out of guilt—let him pay. You can't imagine how hurt and small-minded I was."

Karin is still in love with Bud. She didn't leave Baden. She could have, but she chose to stay. The world is divided between those who stay and those who leave. "It was love. Extravagant love. He thought he could atone for something," I say. For being American, blessed, healthy, innocent, in love. I tell her the story of John, the sister, and Du's sudden departure, my fear of confronting Bud with it.

"If you want me to stay, I will," she says.

As we drive to Darrel's, I don't mention his bizarre proposal to me; the talk is purely of farming or selling, commitment to the land or to the self. "Farm boys grow up guilty if they desert the family ground," says Karin. "It's that simple." This is puritan country; we're born with guilt or quickly learn it. Guilt twists a person, she says.

228

I tell her something I'm expert on: I see a way of life coming to an end. Baseball loyalties, farming, small-town innocence. Most people in Elsa County care only about the Hawkeyes—football or basketball. In the brave new world of Elsa County, Karin Ripplemeyer runs a suicide hot line. Bud Ripplemeyer has adopted a Vietnamese and is shacked up with a Punjabi girl. There's a Vietnamese network. There are Hmong, with a church of their own, turning out quilts for Lutheran relief.

When I was a child, born in a mud hut without water or electricity, the Green Revolution had just struck Punjab. Bicycles were giving way to scooters and to cars, radios to television. I was the last to be born to that kind of submission, that expectation of ignorance. When the old astrologer swatted me under a banyan tree, we were both acting out a final phase of a social order that had gone on untouched for thousands of years.

What I'm saying is, release Darrel from the land. There are different mysteries at work. Bud thinks it's a conflict between farming and golfing, but he's missing the point. Darrel is a romantic, just like him. The banker who steps out of marriage to live with an Indian is the same as the Iowan who dreams of New Mexico. They've been touched with the same virus.

By the scratchy light of a summer sundown, we see Darrel walking the rafters of his hog house. He's rigged strong night-lights with long extension cords, as though he intends to work through the night. Shadow gives us both a good pawing as we make our way to the construction.

"Roof goes on tomorrow. Just getting the last studs in tonight," he shouts down.

No evidence of drinking, of disturbance. He's the appealing kid with the floppy hair. Only a sober man could walk those boards in the dusk, hammering as he goes. "I'd come down and offer you kind ladies a beer, but I'm behind schedule as it is. Plus, if I stop I might never start up again."

Karin shouts up at him, "We just wondered if there's anything we could do."

"The two of you"—He's smiling—"seeing's how you know Bud so well, might work on him for about fifty thousand bucks real quick. Got a lead on a couple-three champion boar hogs down in Burlington."

He executes a jaunty hop to the next joist and begins his hammering all over again. Echoes like rifle cracks roll across the fields.

"Come by tomorrow. Everything's hooked up and I'm letting the hogs loose in here tonight. I reckon we can bank on it not raining."

On the drive back, we can hear the hammering out to the highway, and nearly to our property. "What do you think?" she asks, and I have to say maybe I panicked. He looked like the Darrel of old.

✳   ✳   ✳

230

JASMINE

Bud calls to me. "Jane, hon," he shouts, "it's one of my clumsy nights."

I run out to the living room. Bud's dropped the Financial Statement and Supporting Schedule forms he'd been working on. I collect and sort the papers before I give them back. He looks miserable. It is oppressive in the living room, bugs ping against the black squares of windows. "Honey, I'm a little cold." I throw an afghan on Bud, over his bathrobe. It's his circulation. Bud has changed my life. I am grateful. I am carrying his child. I want to tell him that when I was a girl in Hasnapur only playboys in Bombay movies wore bathrobes. That meant, in shorthand, they had a bathroom, they had modesty, and they had air conditioning. Bathrobes, dark glasses, whiskey, cigarettes: these were shorthand for glamour that we Hasnapuris were meant not to have. I have triumphed. But how can I explain such small odd triumphs to Bud? He's always uneasy with tales of Hasnapur, just like Mother Ripplemeyer. It's as though Hasnapur is an old husband or lover. Even memories are a sign of disloyalty.

Bud has accepted my explanation. The sister had just been discovered and had just arrived; she sent out a call for Du and he's answered it. It might take a few months, but he'll be back for school in September. He worries that we'll never really have Du to ourselves, that he'll always be attached in occult ways to an experience he can't fathom, and as I take off Bud's shoes, I admit there can be no other

231

way for some of us. He is so exhausted he only mumbles, "But not you, Jane, that's what I love about you," and he's asleep even as I unbutton his trousers.

Bud says, "Okay, feed me the numbers under 'Breeding Stock.' What've we got?"

I check the column he wants me to. "Forty sows at two hundred and fifty, which makes ten thousand bucks, and three boars at four hundred, which makes another twelve hundred, so that makes eleven thousand two hundred."

All over Iowa I hear such eerie love calls. Twenty thousand bushels corn @ two-fifty per bushel: make that fifty thousand bucks; four thousand bushels beans @ six even per bushel, so another twenty-four thousand bucks. The Prince of Baden woos the Indian Maiden. I should be swooning by now.

Scaled back, triple-mortgaged, with stipulations to sell off some land and forgo a few improvements, Darrel's loan gets approved. It's well after midnight; the lights are off at Darrel's, and Bud is exhausted. I help Bud to bed. The call to Darrel will have to wait until breakfast. This is a call for Bud, not me, to make. I worry that Bud's call will come too late. Darrel's already imagined himself in New Mexico selling Tandys: his will has muscled out his guilt, or his destiny. He might say take your thirty thousand and stuff it.

Crazy, Darrel wants an Indian princess and a Radio Shack franchise in Santa Fe. Crazy, he's a recruit in some army of white Christian survivalists. Sane, he wants to baby-sit three hundred hogs and reinvent the fertilizer/pesticide wheel. Once the old chemicals have leached from the ground, he talks of cleaning the ponds and raising catfish and giant prawns, of cultivating fancy vegetables on the organic strip, charging premium prices in "Lutz's Corner" of the Hy-Vee.

We call, early enough, but Darrel's not in. Bud decides to deliver the news in person, so after breakfast he rolls down the ramp to my Rabbit, we make the transfer—his arms around my neck as I lift him to the front seat, chair folded in the rear—but he raises his hand before I can start the engine.

"What's that noise?"

There are so many competing farm noises in late July, all of them rising into a single high-pitched whine like the whistling of semi-trailers on the Interstate three miles away, that I'm about to wave it off, until I catch it, too: a skip in the whine, the generalized form of something familiar and specific, as though I had confused something still-voiced and close with something loud and remote.

I remember suddenly the screams of a baby girl thrown down a well in Hasnapur, her cries for two days being taken as prowling jackals across the nullah.

"Hogs!" says Bud.

*　*　*

233

Unfed hogs are like unfed babies. They set up the most pathetic wheezing and whining. Animal abuse of any kind is the one thing a farmer's reputation just doesn't survive. "He better have a good explanation," Bud is saying as we make the turn by the row of maples. The chorus breaks into grunts and squeals. "I told him there's something about a hog that resists all this automation. Cows, yes, they're stupid. But your pig's a plenty smart customer. He wants contact, he wants to see the farmer out there winter and summer, morning and—"

We stop at precisely the same moment. On the road lies Shadow, the halves of his body practically perpendicular. Straight ahead, a boiling sea of pink hogs: their heads, their backs, their legs jump above the open cinder-block wall.

Bud is staring straight ahead at the hogs. I find my eyes slowly rising to the roof's pinnacle. The frail man who is still slowly twisting and twisting from the rafter with an extension cord wrapped around his stiffly angled neck isn't the Darrel, would-be lover, would-be adventurer, who, only nights ago in a cumin-scented kitchen, terrorized me with the rawness of wants. This man is an astronaut shamed by the failure of his lift-off. He keeps his bitter face turned away from the galaxies that he'd longed to explore.

In the car Bud keeps muttering, "Oh, my God! Oh, my God!" and pulling hard at the steering wheel as though he wants me to speed into a U-turn and get us quickly out of earshot of the crazed, carnivorous hogs.

"Tahiti," I sob. "He wanted for us to see Tahiti."

"Jane!" Bud's voice rises harsh above the greedy grunting in the hog house. "Don't fall apart on me!"

"His feet. Bud, look at his feet."

Karin would keep her head. Karin would get the sheriff, fast. She'd phone the family. And comfort Bud. Most of all, she'd comfort Bud. It's Bud who needs Karin's Hot Line now.

Bud's freckled hand closes over mine. Together we turn the key in the ignition. "Good girl," he says. "That's my girl."

I hear gravel chunk against the sides of the Rabbit, but it's not rural routes in Baden I'm racing through. I am deep inside a crater on the moon. Before me huge, lunar hogs leap and chew on Darrel's bloodied boots.

"Jane," my would-be husband begs as I stand by the kitchen window spooning cornbread batter into a baking pan, "light of life, my sweetheart, tell me you love me."

An early ice crusts potholes and crisps the shrubs in our yard. My stomach domes under my skirt. A whole new universe floats inside me. I must not sink. As soon as the cornbread comes out of the oven I'll squeeze into Du's old ski sweater and pace the frosty fields. I shall not think of Taylor and Duff, of what might have been if they really had shown up in our rutted driveway as they'd promised. The last postcard I got from Taylor—his third—said, STILL PLANNING TO COME YOUR WAY. STILL WORKING

THROUGH THE CUSTODY COMPLICATIONS. STILL NEGO-
TIATING WITH BERKELEY. Simplicity is what I envy. It's
been two months since Darrel was buried.

"Jane."

Maybe things *are* settling down all right. I think maybe
I am Jane with my very own Mr. Rochester, and maybe it'll
be okay for us to go to Missouri where the rules are looser
and yield to the impulse in a drive-in chapel. I'm three
months away from what the doctors assure me will be, in
my wide-hipped way, an uneventful birth.

Du is not coming back. He's even dropped out of school
to get a job and help settle his sister, and her husband, and
her children. "Last year a boy, this year a man," he writes.
He's working in a hardware store, learning electrical repair
at night. Carol Lutz wasted no time selling the farm. She
came back to Baden for the funeral, the signing of papers,
and left with a curse on our collective heads.

The first of November, an Alberta Clipper brings a
cover of snow, and with snow come thoughts of Taylor and
Wylie and the trips they took me on. They had met at
Stowe. Taylor had been on a ski team in college, but on
our trips he stayed with Duff on the beginner's hillocks.
Wylie was on the master run all day. One day he outfitted
me, child of the Indian pampas, in a lavender ski suit and
led me through the beginner's run. He said I had the right
stuff. "Next year, Jase conquers the perils of intermediacy,"
he promised, but next year never came. My first winter in

Iowa, right up to the eve of Christmas Eve, Bud and I took up cross-country skiing. We still have those long, lean, elegant skis stored in Mother's basement.

The moment I have dreamed a thousand times finally arrives.

I am in the kitchen, looking south through the dripping icicles. We're no-till, we conserve our topsoil, and we've got a phantom crop of dead corn stalks poking the snow in orderly rows. Trash in the fields has brought the pheasants back and I have a freezerful from generous neighbors. The First Bank of Baden was founded because Bud's grandfather took one look at his son's farm and said he'd fail because he didn't "till to black." He counted trash in the fields as a moral indictment. Bud's grandfather, like most of the old-timers, practically *shaved* his fields, once in the fall and again in the spring. Totally unnecessary, but looked very businesslike. We're puritans, that's why.

A strange car turns in. It's not the old Eldorado. And it's not a government car—that's still my first anxiety—immigration cops don't come in Toyotas. I see two faces inside. After a few seconds and the unbuckling of the harness, one door flies open and a stretched-out version of a little girl I knew, now in blue jeans and a ski jacket, without mittens or a cap, the girl I carried from the parks, that I held on buses, turns to her dad, questioningly, and I see hand gestures from inside, *Go on*, *go on*, they say, and she disappears from my view as the buzzer goes.

I've rehearsed this scene so many nights.

The driver's door opens and Taylor is standing just under my window. He's a giant. On Claremont Avenue he had seemed tall, not gigantic. In the last two years my perspective on things has changed. I have felt tall because the back of Bud's head in the wheelchair comes up only to mid-thigh. I have grown accustomed to the extraordinary.

The giant notes the ramps as he strides toward the front door.

Duff hits the buzzer again, but I wait for Taylor to get to the door before I open it.

Taylor's eyes take me in, the full globe of me. You came too late, Taylor.

"I was wrong," he says, "Iowa isn't flat."

"You came." My voice is hoarse with crazy new longings.

Duff grabs my hands. "Daddy," she says, laughing. "Ask her."

Taylor looks dazed.

"Oh, Daddy, *really*," Duff giggles in my direction. "He was practicing his lines all the way from home." She glides past me into the kitchen.

I wait for Taylor's crooked-toothed grin, but his teeth don't look so crooked anymore. The smile says, *Why not?* "We'll be an unorthodox family, Jase."

He folds me in a hug. It's a cautious hug—I'm too bulky for a full-scale body clasp. Then comes a quick, urgent kiss. "Don't pack," he says, "This is the Age of Plastic."

Duff pretends she's spotted field rats scuttling in the driveway and runs out the door. In her rush, she leaves the door slightly open. Cool winds prickle my face.

"I can't go back with you to New York." Suddenly I know why I haven't married Bud.

"New York's over. We're heading west." Taylor shoulders the door closed.

I lead the way into the living room. "I've never been west of Lincoln, Nebraska."

"We're going all the way to California." He moves around the room, reading Bud's citations.

What am I to do?

I back off toward the window. The window's caulking crumbles as I pick at it. The chilly sparkle of afternoon light tempts. "I have family in California."

Taylor stops in front of the wooden cardinal. "That's quite a prize," he says. Then he says, "You never told me. That you had family in California."

"I didn't have him then."

Taylor bears down on me, confused. "You've already brought a relative over?"

"I can't leave. How can I?" I want to do the right thing. I don't mean to be a terrible person.

"Why not, Jase?" Taylor says. "It's a free country."

Bud's face, gray, ghostly, bodyless, floats in narrowing circles around me. It's the anguished face of a man who is losing his world. I squeeze my eyes so tight that Taylor rushes again to hold me.

Just pull down an imaginary shade, he whispers, *that's all you need to do*. I remember the thick marking pen in his hand printing a confident RETURN on packages of books, records, knife sets I'd thought I wanted. The cord feels dusty.

I am not choosing between men. I am caught between the promise of America and old-world dutifulness. A caregiver's life is a good life, a worthy life. What am I to do?

"I have to make a phone call," I tell Taylor.

From the bedroom I call Karin. "I have to see Du," I announce.

"You've already made up your mind, haven't you?" Karin disapproves, I can tell, though she's trying hard not to sound judgmental. "You're leaving Bud."

Karin stayed. Du and I are different. "I'm not leaving Bud," I explain. "I'm going somewhere."

"You know what you can live with, Jane."

The smell of singed flesh is always with me. Du and I have seen death up close. We've stowed away on boats like Half-Face's, we've hurtled through time tunnels. We've seen the worst and survived. Like creatures in fairy tales, we've shrunk and we've swollen and we've swallowed the cosmos whole. "Yes, Karin."

Karin comforts me. "Don't blame yourself, Jane."

It isn't guilt that I feel, it's relief. I realize I have already stopped thinking of myself as Jane. Adventure, risk, transformation: the frontier is pushing indoors through uncaulked windows. Watch me re-position the stars, I whisper to the astrologer who floats cross-legged above my kitchen stove.

"Ready?" Taylor grins.

I cry into Taylor's shoulder, cry through all the lives I've given birth to, cry for all my dead.

Then there is nothing I can do. Time will tell if I am a tornado, rubble-maker, arising from nowhere and disappearing into a cloud. I am out the door and in the potholed and rutted driveway, scrambling ahead of Taylor, greedy with wants and reckless from hope.